CAPTIVE
OF KADAR

BY
TRISH MOREY

MILLS
BOON

First published in Great Britain 2015
by Mills & Boon, an imprint of Harlequin (UK) Limited,
Eton House, 18-24 Paradise Road, Richmond, Surrey, TW9 1SR

ISBN: 978-0-263-25791-5

Amber could hardly tell him the reason why her lungs had squeezed so tightly in her chest. 'I...' she started, searching for some kind of excuse. 'I don't even know your name.'

He inclined his head. 'I apologise. We seem to have skipped the usual formalities. My name is Kadar Soheil Amirmoez—at your service.'

She blinked, still shaken. 'I'm hopeless with names. I'm never going to remember that.'

He smiled a little—the first time she had witnessed him smile—and shadowed planes shifted, angles found curves and his dark eyes found a spark. And where before he'd been merely striking, with his strong dark looks, now he tipped over into truly dangerous.

Her heart gave a tiny lurch. She had reason to feel fear. And yet still she was glad he'd found her again.

'A simple Kadar will suffice. And you are?'

'Amber. Plain old Amber Jones.'

'Never plain,' he said, in that rich, deep voice.

She remembered the way he'd looked at her across the market, with eyes as dark as midnight, lit with red-hot coals, and she remembered too the warm weight of his hand on her shoulder and the promise his touch conveyed.

And maybe the new, brave Amber wasn't so far away from her as she'd feared.

Because she wanted more.

Desert Brothers

Bound by duty, undone by passion!

These sheikhs may not be brothers by blood,
but they are united by the code of the desert.

Their power and determination is legendary
and unchallenged—until unexpected encounters
with women strong enough to equal them
threaten their self-control…

Read the two concluding stories in Trish Morey's
exciting quartet of searing passion and sizzling drama!

This month meet:
Kadar and Amber in
Captive of Kadar

Look out for:
Shackled to the Sheikh
the final instalment of Trish Morey's
Desert Brothers series
coming soon!

Trish Morey always fancied herself a writer—so why she became a chartered accountant is anyone's guess! But once she'd found her true calling there was no turning back. Mother of four budding heroines and wife to one true-life hero, Trish lives in an idyllic region of South Australia. Is it any wonder she believes in happy-ever-afters?

Find her at www.trishmorey.com
or www.facebook.com/trish.morey

Books by Trish Morey

Mills & Boon® Modern™ Romance

A Price Worth Paying?
Bartering Her Innocence
The Heir from Nowhere
His Prisoner in Paradise
His Mistress for a Million

The Chatsfield

Tycoon's Temptation

Desert Brothers

Duty and the Beast
The Sheikh's Last Gamble

Bound by his Ring

Secrets of Castillo Del Arco

21ˢᵗ Century Bosses

Fiancée for One Night

Dark-Hearted Desert Men

Forbidden: The Sheikh's Virgin

**Visit the author profile page at
millsandboon.co.uk for more titles**

To all the wonderful readers
who have written and e-mailed
asking when they might see Kadar's story.

Thank you so much and here it is.

I love this story—I hope you do too.

Rashid's story, the finale of the *Desert Brothers* series,
will be coming soon!

And to Carol, just because.
Trish xxx

CHAPTER ONE

HE SAW HER in the Spice Market, just another tourist strolling through Istanbul's ancient marketplace, famed for selling spices and dried fruits and a thousand different kinds of tea. Just another wide-eyed tourist, even if she did come complete with blond hair and blue eyes and red jeans that hugged her curves like a second skin.

Not that he was interested.

It was mere curiosity that slowed his footsteps as she lifted her camera to take a photograph of a shop hung with glass lanterns of every imaginable design and colour; nothing more than curiosity that kept him watching as the stallholder took advantage of her stillness, holding out a plate of his best Turkish delight for her to sample. She took a faltering step backwards when she realised she hadn't gone unnoticed, murmuring apologies and shaking her head, setting the messy knot of blond hair at the back of her head and its loose tendrils dancing, but the plate followed her retreat, the eyes of the seller joining in his entreaties for her to just have one *tiny* taste.

Kadar's feet faltered at the stall opposite—it wasn't his usual but he was curious, he told himself, and this shop would do—and ordered the dates he had come to buy for Mehmet, before looking over his shoulder to see whose will was stronger, the stallholder's or the tourist's. The vendor had her attention now, all the time smiling, a toothy smile in a crinkled face as warm as it was persuasive while he continued to engage her, plucking countries from the air as they did here, guessing where she was from—America? England?

As if knowing when she was beaten, the woman gave in, and said something he couldn't make out, but the owner grinned and assured her exuberantly that the Turkish people loved Australians, as she plucked a piece from the plate before her and raised it to her lips.

A long way from home, he registered vaguely, his attention diverted as he handed over a large note in exchange for his dates and was asked to wait a few moments while someone fetched his change. He didn't mind. It was no hardship waiting. The tourist had a mouth worth watching. Her lips were lush and wide and still wearing the shadow of a smile as she popped the sweet into her mouth. A moment later her smile was back in full force, her blue eyes wide with delight and, even surrounded by bright displays of every dried fruit imaginable, every sweetly scented tea and vat of brightly coloured fragrant spice, still she lit up the vaulted marketplace like a lantern.

He felt that smile in a kick of heat that stirred his loins and turned his thoughts primal.

It was a long time since he'd had a woman.

It was a while since he'd felt himself tempted.

He was tempted now.

His eyes scanned just long enough to be sure there was no hint of a partner lurking nearby, and no sticker on her jacket to indicate a tour group nearby ready to swallow her up and spirit her away.

She was alone.

He could have her if he wanted.

The knowledge came to him with the certainty of one who had rarely been turned down by a woman who was available, and after being propositioned by plenty who were not. It wasn't arrogance. Call it history or call it experience, the percentages were in his favour, nothing more.

She was still smiling, her face animated. She was like a burst of sunshine and colour amidst a sea of black winter coats and dark headscarves and she was ready to buy, already reaching into her bag.

He could have her…

And that same unerring certainty that told him he could take her assured him that she would be worth the taking.

Oh yes, she would be worth it.

He could picture himself lazily peeling away the layers that covered her, one by one. Slowly unzipping and stripping away the leather jacket that lovingly hugged her breasts and moulded to her waist, before peeling away those shameless red jeans from her long legs. What layers remained would be similarly discarded until she was revealed, in all her fair-skinned splendour, and then he would unwind the honey-blond hair behind her head and let it tumble down over her shoulders to curl and whisper against breasts plumped and peaked and ripe for the taking.

Her mouth would taste sweet, like the Turkish delight that she'd sampled, and her blue eyes would be dark with heat and she would smile with moistened lips and reach for him…

He could see it all.

He could have it all, and it was all within his grasp…

Then, as if she was aware she was being watched—

almost as if aware of what he was thinking—her eyes fell on him—eyes not just blue, he realised in that moment, but vividly so, almost the colour of lapis lazuli itself. As he watched they darkened, like stone heated over flame, almost as if she recognised him, almost as if she was responding.

She blinked once, and then again. He watched her smile slide away then, even as her eyes turned smoky with recognition as they kept that connection across the bustling marketplace.

Until the stallholder alongside her said something that snagged her attention and she blinked again, and this time turned away. A shake of her head and wave of her hand later, and she was practically fleeing from the market, leaving the disappointed vendor wondering how his in-the-bag sale had gone so wrong.

A tap on his own shoulder saw Kadar presented with his change and an apology for making him wait.

He accepted both the same way as he accepted her vanishing act.

Philosophically.

Because he wasn't interested.

Not really.

After all, he did have plans to visit Mehmet.

Besides, he told himself again, with maybe just a pang of regret, he wasn't looking for a woman. Especially not one who would flee like a startled rabbit.

He left the rabbits to the boys who liked to chase.

In his world, the women came to him.

What the hell had just happened?

Amber Jones stumbled blindly through the market, past shops with their displays of dried fruits and spices and all manner of bright and beautiful souvenirs, ignoring the calls and the banter from stallholders on either side as she passed. Because everything was fuzzy. Nothing was distinct or clear, the sights and sounds of the market that she'd found so fascinating just minutes ago now all a blur. All because she'd been blindsided by a man with golden skin and whose eyes had burned bright like a brazier at midnight.

A man who'd been watching her through those heated eyes.

It had been more than any niggling prickle of awareness—it had been a compulsion that had made her turn her head to catch him staring—and she'd felt the gaze from his dark eyes like a rush of heat—a darkly heated wave that had sent a ripple of promise down her spine and collected in a hot swirling pool deep down in her belly.

Why had he been watching her?

And why had she seen sex in the dark depths of his eyes?

Hot sex.

Jet lag, she thought, searching for logic to lend explanation for the sensation. She was bone weary and operating in a time zone nine hours later than her own. In three hours her body would expect her to be tucked up for the night in her bed back in Sydney, whereas here in Istanbul it was barely time for lunch. No wonder it suddenly felt so crowded in the marketplace. No wonder it suddenly felt so hot.

Fresh air was what she needed—to feel the late winter breeze on her skin and let the sea air cool down her heated, clearly travel-weary body.

She stepped outside the entry to the marketplace, reefing off her scarf and then her jacket, breathing deep

of the cool air as it stripped away her heat and soothed
fractured nerves and calmed a panicked mind.

And with relief came logic and rational thought along
with a little disappointment in herself.

So much for being the strong, independent woman
she'd promised herself she'd be when she'd decided to
venture halfway around the world to follow in her great-
great-great-grandmother's footsteps. Clearly the old
Amber was still lurking, the risk-averse Amber who'd
settle for second best rather than chase after what she
really wanted, if she could be spooked by a look from
just one man.

Because it hadn't been jet lag at all.

It had been *him*, with his face drawn in slashes of
the artist's charcoal.

Him, who owned the space he occupied with such a
supreme confidence, so that the air fairly shimmered
around him.

She shivered, this time nothing to do with the cool
January air, irrationally—*insanely*—missing that sudden flush of heat that had warmed her core and made
her think of long nights and hot sex. How had that happened in just one moment in time? In all the two years
they'd been together, Cameron had never once managed to turn her thoughts to long, hot sex with just one
heated look.

But the stranger in the market had.

How could that even be possible?

And yet his eyes had drawn her, compelling and in-
sistent and communicating to her a dark promise that
her body seemed instinctively to understand—and instinctively to respond to.

A dark promise that had spawned dark thoughts of
all kinds of forbidden pleasures.

No wonder she had run.

For what did Amber Jones even know of forbidden pleasures? Cameron hadn't exactly encouraged creativity in the bedroom. Or in any other room come to think of it. And there were times when he'd fallen asleep alongside her and she'd lain there in the dark and wondered if there wasn't more.

For surely there had to be more.

And then she'd seen more in a stranger's eyes and she'd fled.

More fool her.

Damn.

And not for the first time, she wished she were that strong, independent woman she wanted to be; the way her great-great-great-grandmother must have been, to venture as a young woman of twenty so far from her home amongst the rolling fields of Hertfordshire, in search of adventure in the Middle East all those years ago.

So courageous.

But as she pulled her jacket back on she could see why her namesake Amber had wanted to come. Istanbul was everything she'd imagined it must be. Colourful. Historic. Exotic. She might not be half as brave, but already she could see she was going to love her time in Turkey.

Her stomach rumbled, reminding her that she'd risen and left the hostel before breakfast, sick of slamming doors and a body refusing to sleep when it knew it should be daylight. And there, just across the plaza was one of the carts she'd seen selling bread shaped like bagels and sprinkled with sesame seeds. It would do until she could find something more substantial.

She was waiting for the bread to be bagged when a

hunched old man with a walking stick approached. 'Inglis?' he asked, with a gappy smile in a nut-brown face, with skin that looked as if it were made from leather. 'American?'

'Australian,' she said, getting used to the drill, knowing she stood out as a foreigner with her colouring and dress and that she was an easy target for every street vendor going.

'Aussie! Aussie! Aussie!' he said and his smile became a grin, as if they now shared a common bond. She just nodded and turned her attention to the man with the cart, accepting her bread. 'I have some coins,' the man whispered conspiratorially, as if bestowing upon her a favour. 'Good price. Cheap.'

She barely glanced his way. Sam had a coin collection and she'd promised to bring home her change to add to the few overseas coins her younger brother already had. But she had no wish to buy more. 'No, thanks. I'm not interested.'

'Ancient coins,' he persisted, unmoved, 'from Troy.'

That got her interest. 'From Troy? Really?' That would make a pretty cool souvenir to take home for Sam.

'Very old. Very cheap.' He drew her away from the bread cart and pulled something from his pocket, slowly unwinding his nuggety fingers so she could see the grubby coins resting on his palm. 'For you, special price.'

He named that price as she peered at the two small discs, wondering how she could tell if they really were coins from that ancient city, wondering if Sam would care if they were fake because they looked as if they could almost be real. But they were way out of her price range anyway. 'Too much,' she said, almost regretfully, knowing that her meagre budget would never stretch if she started impulse buying on her first day, only for the man to immediately halve what he was asking.

'Very special price. You buy?'

Wariness warred with temptation. Converted to Australian dollars, what he was asking for now in Turkish lire was a fraction of the spending money she'd allowed herself. She could afford them—*just*—if she didn't splash out on too many other souvenirs. Still...

She flicked her eyes up to his face. 'How do I know they're genuine?'

His free hand crossed his chest, as if she had offended him. 'I plough them myself from the ground. In my field.'

She could believe he had. His hands certainly looked as if they had endured a half-century or more of hard manual work, and his grizzled face seemed honest enough. But still... 'And nobody minds if you dig up coins at an archaeological site? Especially like somewhere famous like Troy?'

He shrugged. 'There are too many coins. Too many for the museums.' He shoved his hand still closer, his brow more creased, and halved the price again. 'Please, I need medicine for my wife. You buy?'

So the rabbit had been snared by a different kind of hunter.

Kadar had imagined her long gone, the way she'd all but fled from their brief encounter, but there she was, talking to an old man across the plaza, those red jeans like a flag and her blond hair gleaming even in winter's thin sunlight, and he once again felt that familiar spike of heat to his groin. He'd bet that if she looked his way, he'd see a matching flare of heat in her blue eyes.

A shame she was so skittish.

He phoned his driver and told him he was ready, while he casually watched the interplay between the old man and the woman, the old man holding out his hand, the girl peering closely, asking questions.

He watched as the old man shook that hand and spilled whatever was in it to the ground, and he watched the way those red jeans stretched lovingly over her behind as she quickly bent over and dived down to retrieve what had fallen. Coins, he figured, frowning. In which case, she'd better be careful. She held them almost reverentially in her hand before attempting to return them to the old man.

He made no move to accept, clearly determined to finalise the sale. Kadar's frown deepened as she shrugged and juggled coins and paper bag and dug around in her satchel for her wallet.

Foolish girl.

He spied his car weaving through the traffic towards him.

Just before he spied the two uniformed men pouncing on the old man and the girl.

CHAPTER TWO

'HEY,' AMBER PROTESTED as someone took her arm, only to look up and find herself staring at a younger man, this one wearing a dark blue uniform of the *polis*. One of two, she realised, the other officer holding the arm of the old man, who smiled thinly while his eyes were laced with fear.

Fear that leached into her bones and made her blood run cold as the coins were taken from her hand and inspected and a nod given in judgement before they disappeared into a small plastic bag.

What the hell was going on?

One officer barked out something in Turkish at the old man and he pointed at her, tripping over his words in his rush to answer.

'Is this true?' The officer's head snapped around to her, his voice as stern as his expression, but at least he had figured enough to address her in English. 'Did you ask this man where you could buy more coins like these?'

What? 'No...'

'Then what were you doing in possession of them?'

'No. I wasn't. He approached me—'

The old man cut her off. 'She lies!' he shouted before following with a torrent of Turkish, angry now and spluttering out his words, pointing ferociously some more at her with his free hand, that caused the *polis* to scowl at her again.

And even though she couldn't understand the language, she knew enough to know it didn't look good. 'You have to believe me,' she pleaded, her eyes darting from one officer to the other, conscious of the crowd that was gathering around them, and she had never felt more vulnerable. She was less than twenty-four hours in a foreign country so very far from home and where she didn't speak the language and fear was coiling tight in her gut. She was the stranger here. What if nobody believed her? They *had* to believe her.

One of the officers asked to see her passport and she scrabbled around in her bag with fingers like toes and her heart thumping frantically in her chest until she managed to unzip the pocket secreting the document. 'You do realise it is illegal to possess Turkish antiquities? It is a very serious offence,' he stated, inspecting the passport.

Illegal.

Antiquities.

Serious offence.

The words collided and mashed in her brain. Why was he telling her this? She'd only picked them up because it was easier for her than for the old man with his walking stick. 'But they weren't mine.'

'Likewise it is illegal to buy and sell them.'

Oh, God. She felt the blood drain from her face. She'd had the coins in her hand. She had been about to buy them.

I didn't know, she wanted to say. *I didn't even know they were real.* And while she struggled for the words to answer, words that might not implicate her further, a new voice emerged from the crowd and joined the fray, a deep and authoritative voice.

No, not just someone, she realised with a jolt as she looked around. Not just a voice.

Him. The man who had been watching her across the market.

He put a hand to her shoulder as he talked, and, breathless and blindsided all over again, she stood there, under the warm weight of his hand, feeling almost— *insanely*—as if the man had laid claim to her.

The old man interrupted at one stage, arguing with him in words she couldn't understand, but the stranger answered back with a blistering attack of his own that had the old man visibly shrinking, eyes fearful as the *polis* scowled.

And even with her heart beating like a drum, even in the depths of panic, it was impossible not to notice how perfectly the stranger's voice fitted him. She hadn't imagined his power before. His voice was rich and deep and spoke of an authority that needed no uniform or weapon to give it weight. He wore authority as easily as he wore his black cashmere coat. And now his thumb was stroking her shoulder. Did he even realise, she wondered, as he continued to make his case, how much her skin tingled at this stranger's touch?

Now, when she shivered, it was not from cold, but from tendrils of heat, curling and sinuous and dancing down to dark places where a pulse beat out a slow, blossoming need.

The voices around her were calming down, the crowd losing interest and filtering away, and even though she was in trouble, in danger of being charged with some kind of crime in a language she didn't understand, somehow she felt strangely reassured by the presence of this man beside her—the very man she'd fled from minutes earlier. And whatever trouble she was in, somehow he had made it so that it was no longer fear that was uppermost in her mind, but desire.

Something was decided. An officer handed back her passport and nodded to them both before the old man was led away between the pair.

'We must go to the station,' he told her, removing his hand from her shoulder to retrieve his phone and make a short, sharp call as the disappointed crowd around them shrugged and wandered away, the show over, 'so you can make a statement.'

'What happened?' she asked, missing the heat of his hand and the stroke of his thumb on her shoulder and that pooling heat between her thighs. 'What did you tell them?'

He glanced around, over her head, as if he was searching for something beyond the crowd. 'Only what I saw, that the old man approached you with the coins and let you pick them up when he dropped them.'

'He had a walking stick,' she explained. 'I thought it would be easier for me.'

'Of course. You were supposed to think that so that you could not pretend they were not yours or that you were not going to buy.'

'But I was going to buy them,' she said glumly. 'I was about to when the *polis* arrived.'

'I know that too,' he said tersely, his mouth tight. He spotted a movement beyond the crowd. 'Ah, here is my car,' he said, taking her elbow. 'Come.'

If his voice had sounded more an invitation than an order—if she had seen his hand coming and been warned of its approach... If either of those had happened, she might have been prepared. She might have steeled herself. But as he gave his command, and took her arm with his strong and certain fingers, it was as if he were not only claiming possession, but also taking control of her, and she knew that if she got into that car with this man her life would never be the same. Something jolted deep inside her then, a fusion of heat and desire and rebellion and fear, and the bag of bread spilled from shaking fingers onto the ground.

He must have felt that jolt move through her, even before she dropped the bread, because his feet paused, and he looked down at her. 'Are you all right?'

She could hardly tell him the reason why her lungs had squeezed so tight in her chest. 'I...' she started, searching for some kind of excuse. 'I don't even know your name.'

He inclined his head. 'I apologise. We seem to have skipped the usual formalities. My name is Kadar Soheil Amirmoez, at your service.'

She blinked, still shaken. 'I'm hopeless with names. I'm never going to remember that,' she admitted, and then wished she had never opened her mouth. He already thought her a naive tourist. Why give him reason to think even less of her?

But instead of the rebuke she was expecting, he smiled a little, the first time she had witnessed him smile, and shadowed planes shifted and angles found curves and his dark eyes found a spark, and where before he'd been merely striking with his strong dark looks, now he tipped over into truly dangerous. Her heart gave a tiny lurch.

She had reason to feel fear.

And still, she was glad he'd found her again.

'A simple Kadar will suffice. And you are?'

'Amber. Plain old Amber Jones.'

'Never plain,' he said in that rich, deep voice, taking her hand, and probably her last shred of resistance along with it. 'It is a pleasure to meet you.'

He knelt down before her and retrieved the bread, now half spilled from its bag onto the pavement scattering sesame seeds and already being eyed by a dozen opportunistic birds. 'You cannot eat this now,' he declared, tossing bread and bag into a nearby rubbish bin, setting birds flapping and squawking desperately in pursuit. 'Come. After you have made your statement, I will take you to lunch.'

And after lunch?

Would he whisk her away and make good on the promise she'd witnessed in his eyes?

Or was she so overwhelmed by all that had happened that she was spinning fantasies out of thin air?

'You really don't need to do that,' she said, testing him. Because she'd seen the tightness in his expression when she'd admitted how close she'd come to buying the coins. He was duty-bound to deliver her to the police station, sure, but he might already be regretting coming to her aid. 'I've taken enough of your time.'

'I have ruined your lunch,' he said solemnly as he ushered her to the kerbside where his car sat idling, waiting for them. He opened the back door for her to precede him inside. 'I owe you that much at least, Amber Jones.'

The way she saw it, he owed her nothing, but she wasn't about to argue. Neither was she planning on running again. He might have made taking her to lunch sound more like duty than pleasure, but she remembered the way he'd looked at her across the market with eyes as dark as midnight and lit with red hot coals and she remembered too the warm weight of his hand on her shoulder and the promise his touch conveyed.

And maybe the new brave Amber wasn't so far away from her as she'd feared.

Because she wanted more.

It was more than two hours before they emerged from the police department into the crisp outside air. A shower of rain had been and gone and the air was fresh and clear after the overheated offices and because it wasn't far to the restaurant, he'd suggested they walk.

Trams dinged and rumbled along the centre of a road forbidden to private vehicles and taxis, making room to hear the call of seabirds wheeling above, and the sound of a dozen different languages on the air around. And then, over it all came a sound she was slowly getting used to, the call of the Imam calling the faithful to prayer, and huge flocks of birds rose as one from the many-domed roof of the Blue Mosque and found comfort in each other from their shared fright, forming an endless circling ribbon of white in the sky.

And it struck Amber in that moment how lucky she was that she was free to enjoy the sight. 'They could have charged me,' she reflected, the shock of her narrow escape setting in as she remembered the stern expressions of the police who'd questioned her and taken her statement. She'd imagined when the police had let her travel with Kadar to the police station that completing a statement was nothing more than five minutes' work, telling them how the old man had approached her, offering coins. A mere formality. She'd been wrong. Dealing in antiquities was clearly not a crime they took lightly in Turkey. 'I thought they were going to charge me.'

'You sound almost disappointed.' He raised an eyebrow as he glanced briefly at her.

Disappointed? *Not likely*. She wouldn't be here

now, watching the birds swirl and wheel to the Imam's prayers. Relieved was what she was. Not to mention a little confused. 'I just don't understand why at first it seemed not such a big deal and then they made such a fuss of it at the station.'

He shrugged. 'What you did was foolish. Of course they needed to make you appreciate the severity of what you were doing.'

Foolish? The judgement stung, threatening to topple all the secret fantasies she'd been harbouring about how this day might progress. She didn't want him to think of her as foolish.

Desirable or sexy, like the way he'd made her feel when she'd found his eyes on her across the marketplace, sure, he could think that. She wanted him to think that.

Not foolish.

'I didn't know there was a law against buying old coins.'

'Surely you do research before you enter a country as a visitor? Surely, if you are any kind of responsible tourist, you find out about their customs and laws before you leave home.'

Well, yes, there was that, then again... 'But they might just as easily have been fake!'

'And you would have been happy exchanging good money for fakes?'

She sniffed. She hated that she sounded so defensive and she hated him because what he said was true. She had been hoping the coins were genuine and of course she would never have considered spending the money if she'd thought them no better than rubbish.

And she would have done her research. Normally. But the decision to come to Turkey hadn't come twelve or even six months ago, and so giving her lashings of time to check out every traveller site going. The decision had been made barely two weeks ago, when she'd had to work out what to do about a cancelled holiday to Bali: stay at home or use whatever credits she could get for her cancelled flights and accommodation towards a trip somewhere she really wanted to go.

Turkey had been a no-brainer. The seed had been planted when she'd come across her great-great-great-grandmother's diary ten years before when she'd been helping her mum sort out her gran's old house back in England, the house her mum had grown up in before she'd moved to Australia. The diary that told of a young girl's excitement about her upcoming trip to Constantinople and beyond, that she'd found bundled together with a pretty bracelet in an old oilskin rag and tucked away in the bottom of a long-forgotten trunk in the dusty attic. Half the pages were missing, so there was no record of her actual travels, and what was left was barely legible, but it was the words a young woman so long ago had penned in ink on the front page—*follow your heart*—that had lodged in Amber's sensible brain.

And whether it was because she shared a name with her great-great-great-grandmother, or because the young Amber Braithwalte's anticipation was infectious, that seed had grown, until she'd known that one day she wanted to experience for herself the exotic capital that had fired up her ancestor's imagination more than a century and a half before.

Follow your heart.

Cameron had thought she was mad to even suggest it.

'Why would you want to go there?' he'd asked her. 'Bali's much closer and it's cheaper.'

'But nobody goes to Bali in January,' she'd reasoned. 'It's so humid.'

'Trust me,' he'd said, and to her eternal shame she'd not only put her dreams on hold, but she'd trusted him, all right. Right up until the time she'd come home early from work and found him shagging her supposed best friend in their bed.

A supposed best friend who'd begged for forgiveness and told her it would never happen again because Cameron wasn't even that good in the sack.

Thanks for that.

No, it was about time she followed her heart. And she didn't have to explain any of that to this man.

'So maybe I didn't have time,' she simply said, downplaying the whirlwind of emotional fallout from the double betrayal that had accompanied that time. It had taken a week before shock and the self-pity had turned to anger, and then it was a no-brainer that she would head to the one place Cameron was never likely to go.

It wasn't until she'd buckled herself into her seat on the plane and taken a deep breath that she'd had clear air to think. So, admittedly, there hadn't been a lot of time to brush up on the finer points of Turkish law or the hazards she might encounter along her journey.

It had been enough to know she was finally fulfilling a dream to visit the country that had bewitched her great-great-great-grandmother more than a century ago. 'Maybe I had other things on my mind.'

'Maybe,' he said, in a tone that suggested he suspected she either hadn't bothered or she didn't give a damn what laws she might break in someone else's country, so long as she got what she wanted.

She gritted her teeth, wondering when exactly the desire she'd witnessed in his eyes had evaporated—in the officious and overheated surrounds of the police station, or when she'd admitted she'd been intending to buy the coins? But did it matter what he thought of her? She'd probably never see him again after today—she'd probably never see him after lunch. What did she care?

Except that she did.

'I'm surprised you'd risk being seen with me, given my propensity to commit random acts of stupidity.'

He actually had the nerve to laugh. 'Oh, I know there's no chance of that.'

It was the laughter more than the certainty that got her hackles up, though the certainty ran a very close second. 'How can you be so sure? You hardly know me. You have no idea of what I might try next.'

'It's the reason you got out of the police station with just a warning.'

Her head snapped around. 'What's that supposed to mean?'

'I heard them talking—there's been a surge in reports of coin sellers and the police are planning a crackdown. There was talk of making an example of you to deter other tourists from trying the same thing. A pretty young tourist charged with trafficking in antiquities—that would get the attention of the world press.'

She gasped. She'd felt she'd come close, but she'd been blissfully ignorant of by just how much. 'So why didn't they?'

'Because I told them that until your departure on your tour tomorrow, I would guarantee your good behaviour. I promised that they would have no more trouble with you while you were my responsibility.'

His responsibility? She stopped dead in her tracks. 'You told them that? Who the hell do you think you are? I don't need someone to be responsible for me. I don't need some kind of babysitter, least of all some man I've barely just met!'

He didn't look remorseful. But then she suspected this man was incapable of doing remorse. 'You would have preferred, I take it, to have been charged and to be languishing right now in a Turkish prison cell?'

Well, *no*. There was that. But still…

'No, I thought not,' he said, reading her answer in her expression. 'Come,' he said, taking her arm in his before she could protest—before she could do anything, really—urging her forward once more along the busy street.

She hated him then for his arrogance. For his supreme confidence that what he was doing was right.

And she hated even more that he was holding her too close.

Much too close.

She could feel him all the way down from her shoulders to her hips, every step they took creating a friction that became more delicious by the second—more evocative—every brush of their clothes giving her another burst of the heat that came from being in close contact with him.

Arousal warred with outrage, and she cursed him for his ability to both infuriate her and excite her. How could it be that his touch wanted to make her lean into this man's strong body, the very man who'd not only insulted her, but quite clearly doubted her integrity and imagined himself some kind of babysitter?

What kind of fool was she?

'So this is actually duty for you, then, taking me to lunch.'

This time it was he who stopped, jerking her to a standstill and snapping her to face him on the side of

the pavement this time, so they weren't blocking everyone's way. 'I take my responsibilities seriously. I said I
would ensure you wouldn't get into trouble while you
were in Istanbul before you join your tour group tomorrow morning, and I will do what I promised,' he whispered, the note in his voice dangerous, his dark eyes
intent and focused hard upon hers, before he paused
and lifted a hand to her cheek and ran the barest trace
of his fingertips down the side of her face, a touch as
gentle as it was electric. 'But who said duty has to come
at the expense of pleasure? Because I suspect our time
together could be quite pleasurable, if you would allow
it to be so.'

The shudder started at her cheekbone where his fingers grazed her skin and reverberated down her body
until it rolled out of her curling toes, its scorching trail
leaving her in no doubt what he was offering.

And then he shrugged and dropped his hand away.
'But if you want me to stop at duty, then just say the
word. If you decide it is not pleasure you wish for, then
I will keep my undertaking to the *polis* and ensure you
do not get into any more trouble before you join your
tour. But I will not pursue you. I am not in the habit of
pursuing unwilling women.'

A tram rattled past, pedestrians walked by spout-
ing words in a dozen different languages, and Amber
blinked at the unfamiliarity of it all. She could scarcely
believe she was standing in the oldest part of Istanbul,
her cheek still tingling from his touch, let alone having
this conversation with this man.

'So,' he prompted, 'what's it to be, Amber Jones?
Duty or pleasure?'

All her life Amber had done the right thing, making

sensible choices, playing it safe, never taking risks. All her life she'd been responsible.

Sensible.

And just look where that had got her.

With an equally safe choice of boyfriend who clearly hadn't valued her and who hadn't turned out to be a safe choice at all.

Her blood fizzed with the possibilities this man was offering. As, if she was honest, it had been fizzing ever since she'd seen him watching her in the Spice Market.

God, she was in Istanbul, exotic, colourful Istanbul, and she might as well have been a million miles from her old life. And maybe it was foolhardy to agree to spend a night with a stranger in a faraway country. Maybe it was reckless.

But maybe it was time to be a bit reckless. Time to pay heed to the excitement in her blood and take a step on the wild side, as her great-great-great-grandmother had been brave enough to do more than one hundred and fifty years earlier.

She looked up at this man, with his golden skin and dark-as-a-hot-desert-night eyes, her heartbeat thumping loud in her chest at just being close to him, and knew that if she played it safe, she'd regret it for the rest of her life.

And her answer came as clearly as the calls of the seabirds wheeling in the sky above.

'Pleasure.'

His dark eyes flared with heat, his lips turned up in approval as he enclosed her hand in his. 'Then pleasure, it shall be.'

He smiled to himself as he led her towards a nearby restaurant that had windows overlooking the park, the glass frontage, he knew, would be filled with colourful dishes, from stuffed eggplants and peppers, casseroles of chicken and chickpeas and lamb, and rice, spiced and fragrant, alongside which lamb and chicken roasted on vertical spits.

So his meek little rabbit had turned out to be less timid than she'd first appeared? She'd fled from him in the Spice Market, and he'd been prepared to let her go.

But there was spirit there, under that nervous exterior, even if he'd had to dig to find it. But it was there, and given the choice again she'd chosen pleasure. At least the time spent babysitting her wouldn't be completely wasted.

Not that he trusted her, despite all her innocent claims of not knowing the laws—after all, what else did foreigners claim when they were caught red-handed but tried to plead ignorance?—but then, he didn't have to trust her. All he had to do was keep her out of harm's way until he got her on that tour bus and sent her on her way and his job would be done.

Keeping her out of the way of illegal street vendors would be no problem given what he had in mind.

Blond tendrils of her hair bounced enticingly on the breeze as they walked, the leather of her jacket brushing against his coat sleeve, and as he turned his head towards her he caught a hint of her perfume, floral and light. He had never been a fan of such scents. He preferred his women dressed in musk and spice and preferably not a lot more, but on her the scent seemed to make sense. Innocent, with a hint of sensuality. A hint of promise.

He liked the fit.

He liked the promise even more.

He smiled. If only his three friends could see him

now, they'd laugh. They'd tell him to be careful, that he was tempting fate. He remembered the last time they'd been together at Bahir's wedding. He remembered the taunts of the two newly married desert brothers. *Who would be next?* Zoltan and Bahir had laughed. *Which of Kadar and Rashid would be next to fall into marriage?*

And Kadar and Rashid had both pointed at the other and laughed.

Of course, the very idea that the two remaining friends would soon follow was ridiculous. Zoltan had married Princess Aisha in order to secure his kingdom of Al-Jirad and Bahir had been reunited with Aisha's sister and his former lover, Marina, along the way. Both marriages had been bound to happen, even if the idea that two of the desert brothers would be married in short order had been unimaginable once.

Well, it had been a good three years since Bahir's wedding and he didn't know about Rashid, but he was no closer to marriage than he'd ever been. And why should he be?

The four men were as good as brothers, bound together by more than blood. They had met while they were at university in the States and, apart from Mehmet, they were all the family he'd ever needed.

And now, while their bond was still strong, he didn't feel any desperate need to follow his friends into the state of matrimony. Marriage was for people who were whole. People who wanted family. But he'd been alone since he was six years old and he was doing just fine. He couldn't see that changing any time soon, especially not when every woman he'd ever met was only too pleased to move right along. So his friends could think what they liked, but if anyone was to marry next, it wouldn't be him.

He wasn't planning on marrying anyone, let alone a woman he'd saved from the clutches of the *polis*.

So he was hardly tempting fate merely spending a night with her.

She was nothing but a pretty tourist.

A short-term visitor to Istanbul.

Temporary.

Perfect.

CHAPTER THREE

THE SCENT OF roasting meat and two dozen delicious-looking dishes wafted out of the open door to tempt Amber, and for a moment she almost forgot that she'd just committed herself to a night dedicated to the pleasures of the flesh. But right now she had more important things on her mind. 'I think I'm starving.'

He ushered her inside. 'You can choose from here or there is a menu if none of these dishes appeal?'

For a woman whose most recent meals had been airline food, fast food or no food at all, she didn't have to think about it. 'No,' she said, mouth watering, in no desire to wait for an order to be prepared when there was such an array before her to choose from, 'this is perfect.'

They made their selections and were shown to a table near a window upstairs while their order was prepared. And then, once again, she was awed—by their vantage point, offering a glimpse of the domed roof of Hagia Sophia with its dancing fountain to one side of the window, and the minarets of the Blue Mosque to the other.

By the man sitting opposite now being greeted by a smiling waiter welcoming him back, a man larger than life with his dangerous dark looks and heated eyes. Long-lashed eyes, she realised as she took advantage of their proximity to study him in more detail. Satin black lashes and long as sin...

And by the knowledge that he'd guaranteed there would be no more trouble with the law while she was under his watch.

Where was the outrage she'd felt when he'd first revealed that little snippet? Had she shrugged it off as easily as he'd discarded his tailored black coat and handed it to the owner who was busy fawning all over him—or simply because of it? Because what lay beneath would blur the edges of any protest. A soft dove-grey knitted sweater lovingly skimmed a chest that could have been carved from stone. *Nice*, she thought, having to drag her eyes away in case they lingered too long, suddenly feeling warm. She unzipped her jacket, and peeled it from her arms, laying it on the chair next to her. The scarf at her neck came off next, tugged out from behind her neck and making her messy knot even messier as more ends worked free. She put a hand to her head, hoping it didn't look as messy as it felt. And then she looked up and stilled when she saw him watching her, his expression deep and unfathomable, and she felt hot and bothered and confused and muddled all over again. 'What's wrong?'

Nothing was wrong. It was all going exactly the way he'd imagined it. Except she'd been the one to peel the jacket from her arms, not him. But just as he'd imagined, he liked what he saw underneath.

He liked it very much.

Her breasts filled the fitted scoop-neck top to perfection without overfilling—without under-filling, for that matter—and he ached to run his hand down the side of her while she lay naked next to him on his bed, down that delicious slope of ribcage to the sudden dip of waist and up the jut of hip to thigh. He longed to drink in her contours through the seeking palm of his hand.

As soon he would.

Their meals arrived and he raised his glass of sparkling water to her, managing a smile over the demanding pulse of need in his groin. 'Nothing is wrong,' he said, even liking the way that knot of hair behind her head was slowly unravelling, those ends floating free or dancing around her face and catching in the light as she moved her head. Bewitching. It would be no hardship spending the night with her.

Just one night.

It had been no selfless act to guarantee she'd stay out of harm's way. He'd keep her so busy in his bed, she wouldn't have time to make trouble. And then he'd wave her goodbye on her tour, turn his back and walk away. And if she chose to get into trouble again, if she chose to mess with Turkish law by taking home a souvenir or two, it wouldn't be on his watch. She would be the tour guide's problem then.

Perfect.

'In fact,' he added, pulling out a smile from his arsenal that he knew from experience women couldn't resist, 'I could not be happier with the way things are turning out.'

Ripples of warmth spread through her at his words, at the heat in his eyes and the slow, sexy smile that spoke of the pleasures of the flesh, reaching places and stirring sensations that made her muscles clamp under the table.

And she so wanted to be bold and brave and confident, like the Amber of old she'd promised herself she'd be, but she was breathless and dizzy and way out of her depth.

His smile grew wider, sexier. His eyes grew dark and burned with intent. 'All I hope,' he added, 'is that you have a good appetite.'

He wasn't talking about lunch. She swallowed. It was disarming. Unnerving. Because she wasn't out of her depth at all. She was drowning in the shallows. Merely trying to hold a conversation with this man was like being tossed by a wave and having to fight foam and sand and salt to work out which way was up and grab a lungful of air for an instant of respite before the next wave rolled her over again.

'I'm famished,' she managed on a whisper, and suddenly she wasn't talking about lunch either.

He gestured towards her plate. 'Please, eat. Enjoy.'

His invitation was a welcome respite, except she'd chosen too much, she realised, for the meal before her was enormous. A glossy red capsicum stuffed fat with meat and rice nestled alongside chicken with okra and a fluffy mountain of white rice on the side. It looked amazing. It smelt amazing. And even though she would have quite happily forgotten all about her meal if he'd suggested they leave and satisfy a different and more demanding hunger, it was a very welcome second best.

As it was, she put a forkful of the rich meat and rice to her lips and closed her eyes as the flavours exploded on her tongue and was in heaven.

'Good?' he asked, and she opened them to see him watching her, his eyes spiced with heat, reminding her all over again of that moment when their eyes had connected and held in the Spice Market.

'Better than good,' she said, feeling suddenly self-conscious. 'Was it that obvious?'

'Don't be embarrassed. I like the way you enjoy what you eat. I like what it says about you.'

Her throat went dry. She took a sip of water, relishing the cool slide of it down her throat, while his eyes didn't leave hers, before asking the question uppermost in her mind. 'What does it say about me?'

'That you are a passionate woman. That you take pleasure in the senses and are not afraid to show it. I like that.'

Sensation careened down her spine. Nobody had ever talked to her as this man talked. Nobody had ever told her that she was a passionate woman. Not even Cameron—thinking back, she wasn't sure passionate was a word he'd possessed in his vocabulary.

But while she was unschooled in knowing how to respond, she knew exactly what the man opposite was doing. He was seducing her, as good as stroking her body with his words, stoking her need with every loaded syllable. 'Who are you?' she said, putting her fork down, thinking the only way she could keep herself anywhere near the surface and oxygen in this mad, tumbling sea was to stop being on the defensive and to try to establish a foothold on the conversation.

'I have told you my name.'

She nodded. 'That may indeed be true, but I don't think it answers my question. Because, you see, you have me at a disadvantage. You heard all my details during that police interview. You know where I live, you know my date of birth, you know everything about me. And yet I know nothing about you.'

'Everything?' His eyes flicked over her, lazy, almost insolent. 'I am sure there are secrets still to be discovered.'

'Stop doing that.'

'What?'

'Stroking me with your words.'

Across the table, he smiled. 'Cats and women. I thought they were both made to be stroked.'

She kicked up her chin and smiled back. 'True. Cats, like women, like to be stroked when it suits them, but when they've had enough, the claws come out.'

She'd been expecting another one of his quick comebacks. What she wasn't expecting was laughter. A deep rich laugh that caught her unawares and shifted the boundaries of the box she'd put him in.

Arrogant and powerful and darkly magnificent, this was a man who could shrug off her arguments and pull her defences apart and set her blood to simmering, all with just a few well-chosen words or a glance from the heated furnace glowing behind his eyes.

There'd been no place for laughter in that picture.

But now there was laughter.

And she liked it.

She liked the smile he sent her even more. 'I did not expect to enjoy this lunch quite as much. So what is it you wish to know?'

'I want to know about you. You're not Turkish, are you? At least, you don't sound Turkish. You don't look Turkish.'

He raised an eyebrow. 'No. Not exactly.'

'And yet the *polis* entrusted me to your care. Why would they do that? Why should they trust you?'

'Perhaps because they know me by reputation.'

She frowned. 'So who are you?'

He leaned back in his chair, his meal, like hers, forgotten for the moment. 'A businessman. I have interests in Turkey.'

'What kind of interests?'

'I support some industries here, that's all.'

'Carpets?'

He gave a brief nod of his head. 'Perhaps.'

'And so you live in Turkey?'

'Sometimes. Sometimes I live elsewhere.'

'Where else? Do you have a wife and children stashed away somewhere? Maybe several wives? Several children?'

He laughed at that. 'No. No wife. No children. And I am not looking for either. Are you finished with your interrogation?'

She shook her head. She was nowhere near done. 'So where are you from, Mr Kadar, if you're not from Turkey?'

'Does it matter where? I am here now, with you. Surely that is all that matters.'

'If you expect me to sleep with you,' she said, getting frustrated by his non-answers, 'I think I have a right to know something about you.'

His eyes gleamed dark with heat. 'I'm sorry if I gave you the wrong impression, but I am not expecting you to sleep.'

Her spine turned molten.

No sleep.

Because they'd be...

And it was only her wrists anchored on the table that kept her upright while she coped with this latest onslaught.

She blinked and looked down at her plate. Picked up her fork. Poked at her stuffed pepper that she figured was only marginally redder than her cheeks right now, the rational part of her brain knowing she'd need the energy if she was going to keep up with this man tonight.

Did she want to keep bickering? Did she really care if he didn't answer her questions and she didn't know where he was from?

She'd already decided to spend the night with him so what the hell did any of that matter? It couldn't change anything.

'I love Turkish food,' she said, her throat achingly tight, knowing she sounded lame and unable to do a single damned thing about it.

'Then, please—' he gestured '—don't let me stop you from enjoying it.'

And with thoughts of seduction swirling in her mind, messing with her head and setting flesh pulsing in secret, aching places, she tried to concentrate on her meal.

Hard though, with the man-god sitting opposite her and with the promise of sex hanging heavy in the air between them. Hard when dinner table small talk was laden with double meaning and heated glances and the electric brush of fingers as they both reached for a piece of bread from the basket.

She waved away dessert so he ordered them coffee as the waiter came to collect their plates. She'd made a sizeable dent in her meal, but, as she'd expected, it had defeated her. But instead of feeling happily satisfied, she was as jumpy as a cat chasing shadows. Where to from here? she wondered.

As if sensing her nerves, he glanced at his watch. 'Are you ready?'

A warm shiver descended her spine. Why did she get the impression he meant ready for bed? Ready for sex? But what else would he mean? Here was a man she'd found an instant connection with on eye contact alone, a man who'd come to her rescue when she'd fallen headlong into a trap set for tourists, a man whose mere touch had sent her senses and her libido into overdrive, and a man she'd agreed to spend a night of pleasure with.

Already she could see a bedroom in his words, the windows hung with curtains in rich jewel shades and a big broad bed with a coverlet spun with gold, and this man the magnet drawing her towards it.

And she wondered at a man whose words contained pictures that possessed the magic to short cut through her brain, shut down her mouth, and feed straight into her need.

Under the table her thigh muscles clenched. 'I think so.'

'Then we should go. It is not far to my apartment. We can pick up your things on the way.'

'My things?'

'It makes sense, don't you agree, given you are leaving early in the morning?'

She licked her lips and nodded. 'Of course, you're right,' she said, wondering how he still seemed capable of rational thought, while all she could think of was bedrooms and sex. But then, maybe he was used to entertaining the occasional stray who wandered inadvertently into his orbit. Maybe this wasn't as unusual a day for him as it was for her.

The thought could have left her cold.

Would have, in ordinary circumstances.

If, that was, she'd been interested in building some kind of long-term relationship with this man. But after Cameron's betrayal, she wasn't interested in long term with any man. As far as she was concerned, one night was perfect. She could indulge her deepest fantasies, maybe even experience a tiny taste of what her ancestor could have experienced more than a century and a half before.

One night with a stranger would be enough.

Enough for both of them, it seemed, because he'd

come right out and said he wasn't interested in more. And whatever his reasons, she couldn't help but admire his honesty. After the experience she'd just had, after all the lies and the deception, it made for a refreshing change.

She stood, reaching for her jacket on the seat alongside her, but he was already up and beat her to it, holding it open for her to slip her arms into. She looked over her shoulder at him as he eased it up her arms and over her shoulders, a smile on his lips, a flare of heat in his dark eyes as if he knew exactly what he was doing to her as his fingers lingered at her neck, his thumbs stroking the skin under her hair, their touch starting spot fires under her skin.

Oh, my God.

What the hell was she letting herself in for?

And why the hell couldn't she wait to find out?

She leaned over and snatched up her scarf and wound it around her neck before she could melt into a puddle from the heat of his touch right there and then, and threw him a hasty, confident and utterly false smile. 'Shall we go?'

CHAPTER FOUR

IT WAS BARELY a hostel, tucked as it was in the back laneways near the ancient city walls, but it was cheap, despite it being located so close to many of Istanbul's famous and ancient sites. She saw him studying the shabby exterior and faded paintwork and knew what he must be thinking. 'Best value in Sultanahmet,' she said, before she held up a hand. 'Don't come in, I'll be right back. It won't take me a minute to grab my pack.'

He didn't argue and she wasn't surprised, knowing that someone like him would have never set foot inside such an establishment and would hardly be tempted to now for fear of contracting some communicable disease or worse.

Hurriedly she gathered the few things she'd left in her tiny shared room, and then did a quick scan of her pack's contents, checking there was nothing missing. Travel itinerary. Toiletries. Then she went sickly cold when she couldn't find her bracelet. It had been there this morning, she remembered thinking about wearing it, deciding against it because it would have been too bulky under her jacket, but it had been here, she had seen it, she was sure she had seen it...

She pulled stuff from the pack, unzipping zips, rummaging frantically and all the while sick with fear. And just as she was accepting that she'd have to report to Reception that someone had been in her room, she pulled out a pair of sneakers from the bottom of her pack and the bracelet rolled out from inside onto the bed. Relief washed over her as she swooped on it, holding it to her chest, remembering she'd tucked it safely away before she'd gone out early this morning.

It was a trinket, nothing more, but it held such sentimental value for her. She'd never forgive herself if she lost it.

And then, because Kadar was waiting for her outside and she'd taken much longer than she'd intended, she bundled everything back in her bag, zipped the bracelet safely into an internal zipper pocket and closed the door on the cheap hostel bedroom. At least for one night.

And what a night it promised to be.

One night with a man who with one look could make you tremble and quake and want for something you'd never known you'd missed.

Until now.

She checked out of the tiny hostel with a myriad questions running through her mind.

Had her great-great-great-grandmother Amber met with such a man? The family history whispered behind hands was that Amber had been kidnapped into white slavery, but had she chosen to stay so long by choice? Because she'd met a man like Kadar with heat in his eyes and seduction in his words?

After today, she could almost believe it possible.

Not that it explained why she had returned to England. So many questions she would never know the answer to. But at least she was here, walking the same laneways and seeing the same sights Amber must have seen one hundred and fifty years ago. How amazing those sights must have been to her then, when she'd been brought up in the rolling green fields of Hertfordshire.

Amber wasn't staying either. She'd be gone tomorrow morning. And given the time she'd spent unpacking and repacking while panicking about losing her great-great-great-grandmother's bracelet, it would be a wonder if Kadar and his heated eyes were still outside waiting for her.

She emerged from the hostel and looked around, heart thumping, unable to locate him anywhere on the busy street, suddenly afraid she'd taken too long and that he'd either lost interest or found some other stray to adopt for the night.

But no, he wouldn't leave her, she remembered. Because he'd promised the *polis* he would watch over her until she joined her tour group. It was only then, when she'd calmed down, that she spotted him standing away to one side a little further away, in the shadow of the ancient wall, busy talking into his mobile phone.

She didn't have to wait to let him know she was ready. He looked up almost as if he'd sensed her watching him, pocketing his phone in the next instant.

And maybe she was imagining it. Maybe she was making castles in the air, but the look he sent her across the street as he pocketed that phone was pure lust and enough to make her body hum and her throat purr.

She'd accused him during lunch of stroking her with his words. Now, as he strode a path between cars across the street, he was as good as stroking her with his eyes.

And she liked it.

Even under her leather jacket, her breasts plumped and firmed, her nipples peaked, the rub of her jacket against her flesh like a sensual caress. Under her jeans, her thighs clenched at the prospect of spending the night with this man.

For a girl who'd only ever believed she could make love to a man that she was in love with, her actions were foreign to her. Reckless, even.

She was about to have sex with a stranger and her body was already humming in expectation of it.

How did that work?

She didn't know. She didn't understand it. All she knew was that she wanted this night and she would have it, to take away as a souvenir of this exotic journey to the east. Maybe just a taste of what her great-great-great-grandmother Amber had experienced all those years before her.

'All set,' she announced a little nervously as he approached, her pack looped over one shoulder.

He unthreaded the pack from her arm and took it from her. 'This is all you have?'

She shrugged. 'I travel light.'

He raised an eyebrow at that. 'Which makes you an unusual woman,' he said, and she smiled, but it was only half a compliment he was offering, because secretly it only supported what he'd already decided about her. He was in no doubt her bag would be a good deal heavier on her return journey, and not just because she would return home with the requisite amount of cushion covers and scarves. He didn't believe for a moment she was an innocent as she made out and there would be plenty of passing street vendors and the trinkets that were on offer to take advantage of before she went home.

Not that he was worried.

If she ventured on the side of illegal again, as he was sure she would before she was done, she'd be someone else's problem.

They made small talk as he led her through the streets and alleyways of Sultanahmet, past tiny coloured timber houses clustered together in the narrow laneways, past stone relics and foundations of more ancient times. And he wasn't Turkish, but he'd lived here long enough that he could provide the history of the area and the stories of Istanbul's long and colourful past. She listened, though he wondered how much she was taking in, because he could sense her nervousness in the brightness of her eyes, and her excitement in her breathless responses.

It amused him. The little rabbit was out of her depth and trying desperately not to show it, but every time they swayed towards each other and their arms brushed, she would jump and catch her breath and lick her lips and pretend nothing had happened.

He smiled. He'd never felt the urge to brush his arm against another's more.

By the time they reached the stately entrance to the restored nineteenth-century building where he lived, she was breathless.

She turned her eyes upwards, taking in the double-level entry with its columns and grand doorway and high arched windows. 'You live here?'

'I have an apartment here, yes.' There was no need to tell her he owned the entire building. She hadn't asked the details and he had no compunction to tell her. She also hadn't asked him what floor his apartment was on.

So it was a surprise to her when the small lift clunked to a stop on the top level, the door that greeted them leading to a spacious and light-filled apartment decorated in rich colours with floor-to-ceiling windows.

'Oh, my God,' she said as she tugged off her scarf,

drawn inexorably to those windows and a view of Istanbul the likes of which she'd never seen. At ground level they'd been surrounded by the streetscape, buildings and trees and traffic. Five levels higher and the streetscape was far below and it was the ship-dotted deep blue Sea of Marmara that was laid out before them.

'Please,' he said, unlatching and sliding open the glass door. 'Be my guest.'

She stepped out onto the wide terrace, and saw that it wrapped around the apartment. Before her and to her right lay the busy shipping lanes, while the view to her left gave a sweeping panorama over the old city and across the Golden Horn. A panorama of red-tiled roofs and minarets and sea and sky. From far below came the sounds of the street, the beeping horns of taxis and the rumble of vans and buses along the narrow streets. And as she watched, the setting sun bathed everything in a rose-coloured glow, turning minarets and clouds alike pink, and when the call to prayer came, the birds rose, they too turning pink as they wheeled and soared in the westering sun.

'Wow,' she said, knowing it was totally inadequate, but unable to find any other words to do the view and the poetry and the sheer wonder of it all justice.

And she sensed rather than heard Kadar behind her.

'Some people say Paris is the most beautiful city in the world.'

His voice was low and rich and she felt his words in the movement of air and the vibration in her bones. She felt them in the sway of hair at the nape of her neck and every part of her tingled.

She felt it all, even though he did not touch her, and

the absence of his touch made her more conscious of him than ever, like an ache that needed to be massaged.

She sucked in air.

In all her twenty-five years, Amber had never considered herself bold. As far as she was concerned, she had been born risk averse.

Sensible.

Boring.

But today, with this man and in this place, and in the shadow of a woman who had been brave enough to venture here a century and a half before, she wasn't going to wait. She turned and lifted her chin and met his dark, impenetrable gaze head-on.

'What do you say?' she asked as if there were any doubt, her voice a bare whisper.

'There is no question,' he said as he tucked a stray wisp of her hair behind her ear and let his fingers linger on her cheek, his touch electric. And his eyes were dark like Turkish coffee, rich and strong, as they searched her features, her eyes, her mouth, only pausing when they found her lips.

'Istanbul,' he said, his voice like a rumble as his fingers trailed down over her jaw and curved behind her neck. 'Istanbul is the most beautiful city on earth.'

His own mouth was beautiful. A wide cupid's bow made masculine. She could watch his mouth form his words for ever. She could listen to his deep voice and play the game of trying to pick where he was from for ever.

He was like the city itself. Exotic. Exciting. Full of mystery and adventure and all of the world mixed together, and he was hers for the night.

Her breath caught, her lips parted as he drew her closer. 'I believe it,' she said, her eyes on his mouth, bare inches away from hers, because there was nowhere in the world she'd rather be right now, than right here, with him.

'Beautiful,' he said, and he drew her closer, his lips slanting across hers, a silken touch, a teasing caress, followed by a kiss so soft and gentle that it left her dizzy and breathless and she would have collapsed against him but he had already wrapped his other arm around her and gathered her close against his hard chest.

And he tasted so good, of spice, and heat and the promise of a night of the pleasures of the flesh.

His kiss deepened, ratcheting up her need as she answered the heady demands of his hot mouth and seeking tongue, as she clung to him, breathless, her head spinning in the whirlwind of desire.

He heard a growl—his growl—as he pulled his head back and she looked up at him to see him frown and his dark eyes conflicted.

'I hope you have a strong stomach,' he said, and his voice was gruff and contained more than a note of bitterness.

She blinked, confused, an ounce of fear wending its way into the warmth of her arousal as she realised. Nobody knew where she was. Nobody but the *polis* who had all but handed her over to this man. And she had nobody but herself to blame for being seduced by the promise in his words.

He was a stranger.

He'd promised pleasure.

But there was nothing to say that his version of pleasure equated with hers.

She shivered. *What did he have planned for her?*

And that flash of fear must have been reflected in her eyes.

'I will not hurt you,' he said, though his voice was barely gentler, as if he realised the fears he had triggered, 'but I warn you now, what you see will not be pretty.'

CHAPTER FIVE

HE'D HAD TO warn her, he told himself.

His usual kind of woman was worldly-wise. His usual kind of woman could forgive anything, be it age, obesity, or deformity, given the right incentive. A night or two in a five or more star resort with all the trimmings. A gown. A trinket. Great sex.

He knew this for a fact.

Because his usual kind of woman blinked and looked away and pretended nothing was wrong and then was only too happy to move on.

This woman wasn't his usual kind of woman. She might not be innocent in the strictest sense of the word, but she was still more ingénue than sophisticate.

That was why she was now biting her lip. That was why she had run from him in the Spice Market.

And if she had run from him then, what would she do when she saw?

Perhaps he should have let her go after all.

But letting her go wasn't an option any more. She was his responsibility and now she had chosen what course she wanted for the night. Pleasure, rather than duty, and he could see in her eyes that she was expecting some kind of perfect night. A night to take away as a souvenir of her trip. A holiday fling to tell her friends about when she got home. She was still nervous and shy, but she had convinced herself that this was what she wanted and she was brimming with anticipation, and so responsive and eager in his arms, her mouth so much like a siren's song, that it had been almost impossible to pull away.

But she was unpractised. Unworldly. And he would not take her to bed without warning her that things might not be as rosy in reality as the light of an Istanbul sunset.

She looked up at him, only the slight tremble in her bottom lip now betraying her hesitancy. 'I'm a big girl, Kadar. I can cope.'

He kissed her then, mostly because she looked so vulnerable and uncertain and only a little because there was a tiny part of him that feared she might change her mind when she saw, and, God only knew, he didn't want her to change her mind. Only to be aware.

'Then come,' he said, ushering her inside, closing the sliding doors on the fading sky. 'And I will show you.'

The day had been intense. The evening was proving even more so.

And Kadar, the man who had moved her, the man who had rescued her, was at the centre of it.

Amber's emotions hovered between excitement and fear, and fear now had the edge. Her body hummed as he shrugged off his coat and took her hand to lead her to the big bedroom.

He flicked a switch and it was just as she imagined. A wide bed with a gold coverlet, drapes in rich jewel colours and Turkish rugs on the floor that brought all the shades of the room together in a splash of silken splendour.

But the furnishings earned no more than a glance, not when it was the man before her that held her interest. He slipped off his shoes and she held her breath, wishing she could do something to slow the beating of her frantic heart.

She had never had a man strip for her before. But he wasn't doing this to excite her. It was challenge she saw in his eyes, rather than desire, as he peeled off his knitted sweater and his trousers and the black band of underwear until he stood naked before her.

No, he wasn't doing this to excite her—but how could it not? Even while she feared what could be so horrible that he must show her, it was impossible to stand impassive while he bared his body to her.

And as each item was removed her excitement grew, and with it her confusion.

Because without his clothes, he was beautiful. His bare shoulders and chest and the hair that swirled a pattern that drew the eye southwards to the nest of dark hair from which his member hung, thick and heavy. A sizzle zipped down her spine.

A sizzle that ended on a question, because it was only then that she realised the welt of skin. The redness. The scar over one hip.

Her eyes lingered, her focus tightened, and, knowing he had her attention, he turned slowly. Breath hissed through her teeth.

His back, from his right hip up to his broad shoulders, was a mess of scarred skin, reddened and angry, pulled excruciatingly tight and wrapped over itself in places, left puckered and swirling in others, as if it had melted and been stirred and left to set.

Whatever had happened to this man had happened a long time ago and had been shockingly brutal and she could only imagine the pain he must have suffered not only then but in the months and years afterwards.

'Do I repulse you?'

She looked levelly at dark eyes cast over his shoulder.

'Do you want me to be repulsed?'

He spun around. 'What?'

'You're burnt. Scarred. It's impossible not to notice. So now that I have noticed, do you want me to ask how it happened, or to ignore it?'

'Ignore it.'

'Fine. Then that's what we will do. And in that case,' she said, with her hands at her jacket, 'I think one of us in this room is overdressed.'

It was the most brazen thing she'd ever said. A second later her jacket was flung to the floor and that was the most brazen thing she'd ever done. Until she followed it with her top and boots and jeans and stood there less than a minute later, in her perfectly serviceable, totally unsexy underwear.

That was when she faltered, wrapping her arms around her midriff and looking up at the ceiling. Good grief, what was she thinking, making out as if she were some kind of striptease artist? She was way out of her depth. Way out of her league.

It was his hands that tugged her arms open. 'Why did you stop?'

She shook her head and lowered her eyes to his. 'I'm no good at this. I can't pretend to be something I'm not.'

'No good?' he said, and took one hand, and guided it to his erection, hard and wanting. This time air rushed into her lungs. She looked down as he bucked under her hand. God, he was so beautiful. So big and rock hard. 'Do you still think you are no good at seduction?' She blinked up at him as his hands reached behind her and eased free the tie holding her hair, letting her hair tumble over her shoulders. 'You are a beautiful woman, Amber. Beautiful and desirable. Believe it.'

With this man's hands in her hair, with her hand cupping the weight of his thick erection, she almost could. And then he kissed her again, and his hands skimmed over her shoulders and back and he was easing her bra straps down her arms and air stroked her breasts and tightening nipples as her bra fell away.

She gasped into his mouth as his hands encircled them, unable to stop herself from trembling, while his thumbs stroked her nipples, coaxing them still harder, and her senses buzzed and sparked, and the aching space between her thighs pulsed with an unrelenting need.

God, had she felt this breathless before? This utterly boneless?

He scooped her into his arms, as if sensing her weakness and her nervousness, but confusing her when he bypassed the bed. 'Where are you going?'

'We have the entire night. There is no rush. A shower will relax you.'

Her body sizzled at the thought. She'd be surprised if she didn't damn well steam when the water hit her skin.

The bathroom was like nothing she'd ever seen before. There was a huge shower stall with a marble shelf on three sides and a big basin carved from alabaster under a tap that he started to fill. A decorative metal dish held a block of soap and a rainforest showerhead sat above.

And then he pulled what looked like a pair of tea towels from a rack, only longer. One he lashed around his own waist. The other he slipped around her back and tied it at the front over her breasts.

'Have you ever had a Turkish bath?'

'No.'

'You should, before you go home. An afternoon spent in the *hamam* is not to be missed. But until then, let me give you a taste.'

He slid his hands under the cloth. 'But we can dispense with these,' and he slipped his fingers into her panties and slid her perfectly serviceable and utterly boring underwear down her legs.

And she wasn't naked, not technically, even though the cloth was short enough to be considered indecent and left her legs bared to his gaze, but the combination of his touch on her skin and the knowledge that there was nothing more between them than a few threads of cotton set her skin tingling.

He drew her into the shower stall and sat her on the ledge while he dipped the metal dish into the wide bowl, testing the temperature before tipping the bowl slowly over her shoulders.

The water flowed over her in a warm rush and he filled the dish again, and lifted her chin and poured water over her face and head, scrunching her hair, repeating the action until she was drenched.

And then he took the soap, olive-oil soap, he explained, and soaped her arms and shoulders , rinsing it off with another dish of water.

There was something very sexy, she realised, about a man wearing only a cloth knotted low at his hip when his muscles moved so clearly under his skin as he worked. Especially when that cloth was distended by what lay beneath. It was sexier than if he'd been naked.

Was that how he felt? And then she glanced down at the now sodden cloth, to see it plastered to her body, her breasts, her waist and the jut of her nipples plain to see.

Kadar finished with her arms and knelt down and

started work on her feet and legs, his hands slippery with soap, massaging circles up her calves and over her knees and higher to her thighs.

She reached for him and he stilled her hands, putting them down on the ledge. 'Sit,' he told her. 'Be patient.'

It was a torture of sorts, this slow deliberate assault on her senses, as his fingers came achingly close to her core and her muscles clamped down.

He knew what he was doing to her. He knew and he smiled and placed that leg down and started working on the other.

'You're a cruel man, Mr Kadar.'

He smiled and massaged his thumbs into the arch of her foot until she cried out with the pleasure and the pain before he shifted his attentions to her ankles. More water. More soap. More slide of skin against skin past her knee, until once again he was stroking her inner thigh, stoking her need.

And took his hands away again and she had to stop herself from whimpering as he took the soap and spun it in his hands, the smile in his dark eyes almost wicked as he reached his slippery hands to her legs and slid upwards, and this time he didn't stop.

She gasped when his thumbs brushed her curls but his smile only widened and his thumbs didn't stop there. They made lazy circles over her mound while his fingers continued to caress her thighs. Those thumbs ventured mercilessly lower, and still lower, so achingly close and yet nowhere near close enough for the need that he was building inside her.

'Oh, God,' she said. 'We do only have one night.'

And he laughed, low and husky, but something in her appeal must have worked, because his slick fingers joined the game and her thighs opened on a long sigh, the stroke of his fingers like a precious gift.

And somewhere in the waves of sensation building inside, it occurred to her that if this was foreplay, then she'd been missing out a whole lot of years.

She blinked half-shut eyes open, half-drunk-with-sensation eyes trying to focus as she watched him take a dish of water from the basin and pour it between her parted thighs, a slide of warm water against sensitive flesh, sluicing away the soap.

He smiled at her then, and she thought how hand-some he looked through her sex-addled eyes and how pleased he looked with himself and that now that she was so relaxed and less nervous he would no doubt make love to her.

God, his fingers had been fantastic there, but it was him she wanted, deep inside her.

Except he didn't make love to her. Not with the part of him that was still pushing hard under his own cloth.

Instead his smile widened and he pushed his arms under her legs and pulled her closer to the edge of the ledge and dipped his head down.

She tensed, and reached for his head. 'No!'

'Why?'

And she'd been about to say that Cameron had never—could never—except she felt the flick of this man's tongue against her tender flesh and sensation unplugged her brain. It was either that, or the crack of her head hitting the tiled shower wall as he drove her wild.

There was no pain. Only pleasure. Because nothing could detract from the mounting pleasure of his tongue working magic, of his lips tugging and teeth nipping so gently but, oh, so purposefully. As his fingers played at her entrance and his lips tugged on her most sensitive flesh and his fingers slid inside and there was no holding it back and the storm was upon her.

He pulled her face down to his and she came, clenching around his fingers, kissing lips that tasted of him and tasted of her, as she rode out the storm front.

She clung to him as the shudders subsided, feeling suddenly guilty and gauche and so unpractised. 'I'm sorry,' she panted. 'Apparently I couldn't wait.'

The sound of his low laugh rumbled against her, rumbled through her. 'Don't be sorry,' he said as he pulled himself away and and coaxed her to her feet.

She stumbled against him. 'I don't think I can stand.'

'You don't have to,' he told her as he turned her and had her kneel with her back to him on the wide marble ledge.

She went willing and breathless, her body still humming. Whatever happened now, she reasoned, was all for him and she would do her best to make it as good for him as it had been for her.

Although it had been so good…

One of his hands slid up the length of her back to her shoulder, the other sent seeking fingers to her core.

There was nothing for her spine to do in response but to arch and curve into his touch. He groaned then, as if she were the one torturing him, and then she felt the press of him there—right there—where his fingers had been and exactly where she had wanted him from the moment he'd offered this one night of pleasure.

A connection she'd sensed from the very first moment their eyes had connected across the Spice Market.

His hands anchored her hips, and she felt her tension mirrored in his as he hovered and kept her there, waiting on the brink.

He gave a strangled curse and pulled away but before she'd turned he was back, the foil packet ripped asunder, the rubber already rolling on, and he was back. Mercifully back, his hands holding her hips steady as he slowly and purposefully pushed into her.

Her head lolled back as he filled her.

Filled her and lingered, his body against hers, inside hers, the connection complete. She tried to cling to him while he withdrew, and hold him there, for he was almost gone, when he thrust into her again, deeper this time if it were possible. And then again. And then his hands left her hips and stroked her breasts and teased her nipples and she whimpered with need while her hands lay flat on the tiled walls. All she could feel was desire.

And want.

And need.

How did that work? Surely it was impossible for a woman who'd just been blown apart by the touch of a wicked tongue and clever mouth to feel that coiling, building spiral of sensation again so soon?

But no. Not impossible. Not now. Not with this man.

He pumped faster. Harder. His ragged breathing bouncing off the tiled walls. His mouth was at her throat, his hands squeezed her breasts and his hips slapped against hers and somehow the impossible happened, because for the second time in one day she felt her need building and spiralling and focusing until all there was was this man feeding her need and the only thing she wanted was more and the only place she wanted to go was higher.

He touched a fingertip to that sensitive nub of nerve endings and gave her more.

He took her higher with each deep thrust.

Until she could take no more and there was no place

left for her to go but to shatter like a wave crashing on rock. She heard a cry of release and recognised her own voice. Kadar went rigid behind her and she heard another cry, coarse and triumphant and his, as he found his own release.

He slumped over her, his mouth at that sweet spot where her shoulder joined her neck, his choppy breathing fanning her skin. With a final parting kiss to her skin, he pulled free and snapped on the shower. Within a few moments the shower stall was filled with steam and he helped her from the ledge and held her as the water cascaded down over them both.

He didn't talk and she didn't expect him to. She was happy with silence. Because while her legs were weak, her knees were sore, and her body felt spent, never before had she felt so alive in the knowledge of what her body was capable of.

And she made a vow to herself right there and then, as she lifted her face up to the stream of water, that never again would she settle. Not now that she knew what was possible.

He should be angry. He was angry, but with himself. Not since he'd been a teenager had he come so close to having sex with a woman without using protection.

What the hell was wrong with him?

Thank God she didn't seem the kind of woman who wanted to make small talk after sex. He snapped off the shower and handed her a towel and so what if he was a little brusque as he passed it to her? He had things on his mind.

What had he been thinking? One minute he'd been in control and pleasuring her the way he knew women

liked to be pleasured, and the next he was almost for-
getting the most basic of rules.

Thank God his friends—Zoltan and Bahir and
Rashid—would never find out. They would love that
if they knew. They'd have him married off. Written off.
Same thing really.

He threw his towel on the floor.

It was just a mistake. It had been a while and the sight
of the curved perfection of the sweep of her bare back
had momentarily side-swiped his brain. That was all.

It wouldn't happen again.

'Are you hungry? Do you want anything to eat or
drink?' he asked as she towel-dried her hair.

Her hands paused and she blinked up at him with
her beautiful blue eyes, her wet hair tousled and curling in tendrils around her face.

Medusa, he thought, with the power to turn a man
to stone. That would explain it. And then dismissed the
thought as ridiculous in the next breath.

'I could do with something to drink. Coffee?'

'Make yourself comfortable in bed. I'll bring some.'

Night had fallen while they'd been in the shower and
now the black sea was lit with the lights of ships and a
silver glow from the moon.

She was in bed when he returned, the covers pulled
up over her breasts, but it wasn't that that threw him. It
was that she was even here. He wasn't used to women
being in *his* bed. Rarely if ever he'd bring a woman back
to his apartment. Never he'd entertain the thought of
her staying until morning.

And yet this woman was staying until morning.

Only, he reminded himself as he put the tray down
on a side table, because she was leaving early to join
her tour group.

He wasn't making an exception, so much as adapting to circumstances.

It didn't mean anything, no matter how good she looked there.

'This is service,' she said, scooting up higher in the bed, her arm modestly holding the covers over her breasts.

And *that*, he realised, was the difference right there.

His usual kind of women didn't do modesty. They were all about advertising their wares, even when he told them he wasn't in the market to buy, in the hopes they might convince him to change his mind.

He'd never change his mind.

He put a tiny cup of coffee and a glass of water beside her, and offered her the Turkish delight.

'Oh, I love this,' she said, taking a piece and clearly savouring it as she put the sweet in her mouth.

'I know,' he said, when she looked up at him questioningly. 'I saw you in the Spice Market, remember? I remember the look on your face when you tasted some.'

'Oh.'

She turned her face away and reached for her coffee, but not before he'd got the distinct impression she was blushing. A woman in his bed blushing. He shook his head. It was turning into a night of firsts.

She sipped her coffee and kept her gaze averted and he was compelled to ask.

'Why did you run from me?'

Her head wheeled around and yes, he'd been right, because there were the telltale red stains on her cheeks. 'What?'

'In the Spice Market. Why did you run?'

'I didn't—' she began, her eyes wide with denial, before she saw his raised eyebrow and turned her eyes up to the high ceiling. 'Okay,' she said with a shrug, 'I can see it might look that way. It's just that you startled me a little. You looked so…'

She paused mid-sentence, her teeth scraping her bottom lip.

'So—*what*?'

'Intense.'

He smiled. Intense was exactly what he'd felt the moment she'd smiled. 'You have a unique beauty. It is hard not to stare at you.'

Her eyes were wide and lit so brightly blue, her cheeks flushed, her lips pinked and slightly parted and his groin ached anew.

'You're doing it again,' she said, sounding suddenly breathless.

And he took her hand and pressed the back of it to his lips. 'I know.'

She gasped and he felt her tremble under his lips.

'Is that why you did it?' she whispered. 'Is that why you got involved back there, with the coin seller?'

He shrugged and kept her smooth-skinned hand in his and thought about how close he'd been to getting into his car and how he would have left without a backward glance if not for the arrival of the *polis*. And even then, he hadn't interceded on her behalf with any ulterior motives.

They had come later, when the *polis* had wanted a guarantee and it had occurred to him that there was one sure way he could keep her out of trouble…

'I do not like to see people taken advantage of,' he simply said. 'Especially when they cannot speak the language.'

'So you hang around the Spice Market saving tourists from being ripped off. That's very noble of you.'

He smiled. For all her shyness, for all her inexperience, she wasn't a complete mouse. 'Well, perhaps I am selective in whom I choose to help.'

'So why did you choose to help me?'

'Because you don't speak Turkish and you were at a disadvantage.'

'Oh.'

It was one of those disappointed *'ohs'*. The ones women gave when they'd got the wrong answer to their question. And in spite of the fact he owed her nothing, that he was already doing her a favour and he had no need to stroke her ego, he curled an arm around her neck and drew her close.

'You know why I chose you.' He pressed his lips to hers, and tasted coffee and Turkish delight and the essence of woman and his body stirred. 'Because I wanted you.' Her eyes were wide, her lips parted as he pushed the covers from her perfect breasts and curled his fingers around one, his thumb teasing one nipple into bold relief. 'Because I knew it would be good.' Her breath hitched as he sent his hand southwards, skimming the slight undulations of belly and hips and between her legs as his hand parted her. She gasped as his thumb circled that tightly bound nub of nerve endings while his fingers found her slick and ready.

He reached for a condom and in the next movement pulled her astride him, positioning her and drawing her down his length as breath hissed through his teeth.

'And I was right.'

CHAPTER SIX

THE NIGHT WAS short and morning came too soon. He watched the sun rise from the terrace, saw its coming light wash the sky pink above the hills and apartment buildings lining the shores of the Golden Horn, before it burst free of the land and blazed red into the winter's day.

Too soon.

But he could not stay with her in bed. The urge to hold her had been too strong.

He did not hold women in the morning. This was new to him. Uncomfortable. Discomfiting.

But then he did not entertain women who did not bat an eye at his scars, who recognised burns for what they were, and who asked him if he wanted to talk about it. Of course, he had no wish to talk about it. But he wasn't used to being asked.

He looked at the watch he'd slipped on his wrist before stepping out in his robe onto the terrace. It was time she was up. He turned to go inside and make coffee.

It was just as well she was leaving.

She woke alone, confused at first, until she remembered where she was and in whose bed.

But alone, the mattress beside her cold.

So he had taken his fill of her? She sighed.

So be it. She picked up her watch and checked the time. Today she left Istanbul on her tour and she was excited about that. Really she was, even if her excitement was blunted at the thought of leaving this night and this man behind.

For the night had been one revelation after another. There was nothing, it seemed, that this man could not do with his clever mouth and his skilful fingers and his...

Oh, God. She shivered, remembering the feel of him sliding into her. Sliding out.

Delicious memories she could take home.

Memories against which all future lovers would no doubt be judged. It wasn't such a bad souvenir.

And the tour was why she was here. To follow in the other Amber's footsteps and visit the sights of Turkey and some of the places she'd been so excited about visiting more than a century and a half ago. And if she found something that linked her great-great-great grandmother to this country somewhere, something that might explain those missing years that were probably described in the pages that had been torn from her diary, that would be the bonus.

She was already showered and dressed, her crazy bed-head hair tamed in a knot behind her head, and folding the last of her things into her pack when he came in with coffee.

'In a hurry to leave?'

She smiled. He almost sounded annoyed she was almost ready. She knew he wasn't. Whatever pleasures of the night they'd shared, he would be more than happy to get rid of his charge, having faithfully discharged his duties. 'I thought you'd want to be rid of your obligation as soon as possible.'

'You're not expected at the tour office until eight.'

She shrugged. 'I don't mind getting there early. There'll no doubt be others waiting who I can talk to. I might as well get a head start on meeting my companions for the next few days.'

He grunted. 'As you wish.' Then he headed for the shower.

She sipped her coffee thoughtfully.

Well, she hadn't expected him to try to talk her out of going early and he didn't disappoint. She'd been a distraction for a night for him and he was no doubt wanting to get rid of her and get back to his life.

The morning was cold, dark coats and wool scarves the order of the day. And even though she protested, he insisted on buying her yoghurt and zucchini fritters for breakfast with freshly squeezed orange juice, and some bread for the trip. Duty, she told herself. He'd taken his pleasure and it was all about duty now.

'Thank you,' she said as she tied her scarf around her throat and they headed out onto the street, the clang of tram bells and the call of sea birds heavy in the thick cold air.

He shrugged. 'It was only a light breakfast.'

And she smiled. 'No, I mean, thank you, for last night. For everything.'

'It was my pleasure.'

She shook her head. 'No, I rather think it was mine.' He smiled at that and offered her his arm, one last gesture, one last touch, and she took it.

She would miss Kadar. He'd rescued her. He'd educated her. He'd shown her that there was an entire world of sexual experience out there that she'd only ever glimpsed at, and she wasn't going to settle for average again.

There was a crowd gathered around the shopfront
of the office where she was due to meet her tour. She
glanced at her watch. It was only a few minutes before
eight. 'Surely they're open by now?'

Kadar's eyes narrowed. Someone was yelling. A
woman was crying. A young man was pounding on
the door with his fist. There were so many people and
it was impossible to know who was supposed to be
joining the tour and who had stopped to watch the
proceedings.

He spotted a local man standing on the periphery and
asked him in Turkish what was happening.

He took a drag of his cigarette and pointed to a sign
on the door, almost hidden amongst the travel posters
featuring shots of Ephesus and Pamukkale and more.

'What is it?' she asked as he peered over heads to
read the sign.

'The tour is cancelled,' he told her. 'The tour company offers its "sincere apologies to its clients" but is
unable to keep trading. So your tour—and all tours cur-
rent and future—is cancelled.'

'Cancelled? But how can it be cancelled? What about
my money? I've already paid.'

'Do you have travel insurance?' he asked her.

'Of course. But—'

'Then you need to contact your insurer immediately.'

'But what about the tour? I've paid for eight days'
travel and accommodation. What am I supposed to do
now?' She looked up at him, searching for answers, and
then shook her head as she remembered what he was
doing here. Dropping her off. 'Oh, forget it. Not your
problem. You might as well go. I'm sure someone will
sort something out.'

'I'm not leaving.'

'There's no point staying.'

'I will not leave you here in the faint hope that some-one will sort something out. Chances are, nothing will be sorted out, and you will have to make alternative arrangements.'

She felt a tiny frisson of warmth. Maybe he had felt something for her after their night of pleasure. Maybe he wasn't so keen to be rid of her after all.

She smiled. 'Thank you. That's very sweet of you.'

'It's not sweet. I told the *polis* I would be respon-sible for you while you were in Istanbul. While you remain here, for whatever reason, you also remain my responsibility.'

He might as well have thrown a bucket of cold water over her. 'Duty,' she snapped.

'Duty,' he agreed. 'But you yourself have seen, duty and pleasure need not be mutually exclusive.'

She shook her head, not sure that was such a good idea. One night had been their deal. One night, and she could manage to walk away knowing it had to be this way and feeling only the slightest pang of regret. But to stay longer in this man's company? In this man's bed? When it was obvious that he neither meant it nor wanted it. 'No, there's no need. I'm sure someone will be here soon to sort something out.'

'I just did. We will leave your contact details with someone in the group. If something is resolved, they can let you know. Meanwhile you will come with me.'

She didn't want to go with him. She might have wished their one night together had been longer, but she didn't like him assuming he could tell her what to do. She'd had enough of people telling her what she could and couldn't do. That was half the reason she was in Istanbul. 'No, I am not going with you.'

'And if I tell the *polis* that you refused to co-operate and they decide to press charges after all?'

Heads turned and she cursed him under her breath as she pulled his arm around so their backs were to the crowd. 'You wouldn't dare,' she whispered.

'I am responsible for you. If you wish to go it alone, I will have no choice but to let them know. In case you come to the authorities' attention again and they blame me for not doing as I promised.'

'I am *not* going to get in trouble again.'

'How do I know that?'

'Because I told you.'

'And you also told me you had been intending to buy those coins. An illegal act. Now do you understand why I cannot trust you alone?'

'Go to hell!'

'I'm sure that can be arranged. But rest assured, if that's where I'm going, you will be accompanying me.'

She rolled her eyes and caught sight of a woman nearby watching them, their conversation clearly more interesting than the student pounding on the door or the man yelling or the woman rocking on her haunches and wailing melodramatically.

'He's my uncle,' Amber explained, 'married to my mother's sister and he thinks he rules the world.'

'She's my recalcitrant niece,' Kadar said, 'and if a tour bus turned up right now, I would gladly throw her bodily onto it.'

The Canadian woman jerked her head towards the wailing, yelling, fist-thumping members of the group. 'That would be a pretty reasonable punishment. I'm beginning to think I may have just been saved from the tour companions from hell.'

And then she reached for Amber's arm. 'Sweetie,

take my advice and go with your uncle. Anything's better than being stuck with this lot. Sure I might prefer to count my money, but I'm counting my blessings already.'

'You should listen to your new friend,' Kadar said. 'She makes a lot of sense.'

'Thank you, *Uncle* Kadar. It seems I don't have a choice right now.'

'No,' he said. 'You don't.' He passed Amber's contact details on to the Canadian woman and asked her to call if she learned anything. Then he took Amber's arm. 'Shall we go?'

What choice did she have? 'He's not really my uncle,' Amber threw over her shoulder as they left.

'I know,' the woman said with a smile. 'Lucky you.'

She didn't feel lucky. Her tour had been cancelled and unless she got some emergency assistance from her travel-insurance provider, she'd done the bulk of her travel money, and meanwhile she was stuck instead with the babysitter from hell. And he might be amazing in the sack, but there was more to life than great sex.

Wasn't there?

'Where are we going?' she asked, when they turned right instead of left where she was expecting.

'To visit a friend.'

'I need to call my insurance company.'

'It can wait half an hour, can't it?'

She licked her lips, the spark of an idea flaring into life in her mind. 'But do I need to come with you? Why can't I just go back to your apartment and start the ball rolling? Surely the sooner I notify them, the better?'

He thought about that for a moment. He'd promised to see Mehmet and he'd already put it off once, because of this woman. He'd waited because he'd figured he'd be done with her by now. And he'd much prefer to see his old friend without this woman in tow. Mehmet might be blind, but he had a way of imagining things that weren't there.

He had to admit, her offer was appealing.

'You remember where the apartment is?'

She shrugged. 'Of course. It's not far.' She pointed down the street to their left where she'd been expecting him to turn. 'Right at that next corner and left at the carpet shop.'

His eyes narrowed. 'All right,' he said, reaching for his keys. I'll meet you back there, then.'

She took the key and turned to go, her eyes so bright that the restless alarm bells in his mind rang out loud and clear. This was a woman who should never venture anywhere near a poker game.

She stopped dead when he grabbed hold of her pack. 'But I'll take this. Save you carrying it.'

Her face bleached of colour. She looked at the bag. Looked up at him, a war going on behind her eyes. Finally she glanced down at her cross-body bag and seemed to make a decision. 'Okay,' she whispered, and slipped the pack from her shoulders.

'Oh,' he added, because that had been too easy, 'And your passport. I think I'll take that too.'

Her chin kicked up. 'Why on earth would you want that?'

'If you're just going to the apartment, it's not like you'll be needing it.'

'You don't trust your own niece, *Uncle Kadar*?'

'That's just it, my recalcitrant niece,' he said as he hauled her pack over his shoulder and took back the key from her hand. 'I don't.'

* * *

Mehmet lived in a ground-floor apartment tucked away
behind the lift lobby of a nineteenth-century apartment
building. If the noise and grind and endless pinging of
the single lift had ever bothered him, he didn't let on.
Kadar suspected he liked to hear the comings and going
of his neighbours, even if he couldn't see much of them.

He had the dates he'd bought in the Spice Market in
his pocket. The trouble was he had an unwilling and
sulking visitor to accompany him too.

'Mehmet is old and mostly blind,' he said, 'and may
or may not choose to speak English, although he understands it perfectly.'

'It's okay. I won't say anything.'

'He'll know you're there, even if you say nothing.
He sees more blind than most seeing people see with
their eyes. He'll be curious why you are with me. I will
tell him the truth, that it is only because your tour was
cancelled while we make alternative arrangements.'

Amber had no issue with that. 'Tell him what you
like. It makes no difference to me.'

He turned his head to her. 'In that case, I will tell him
we spent a night of unbridled passion in my bed and
that in the morning you begged me not to let you go.'

She snorted and didn't care in the least if she sounded
unladylike. 'Dream on,' she said. 'If he can see so much,
he'll know that's a lie.'

He stopped halfway across the tiled lobby and turned
to her. 'Where do you get this from, this bravado?
You are inexperienced sexually, in no way could it be
said you are worldly-wise, and you bolt at a stranger's
glance, and yet you have this streak of defiance that
comes from nowhere.'

She didn't know herself. But maybe after playing it

safe her entire life and the disaster that was Cameron and being bossed around by this man who insisted on babysitting her, she was starting to discover what she actually wanted.

'Maybe I'm just sick of being pushed around.'

He put the fingers of one hand to her chin and lifted it even higher, her chin rigid, her eyes sending him daggers. 'Save your passion for bed. We may be forced into each other's company for longer than either of us desire, but we need not waste the nights.'

He let go of her chin and turned and headed for the door on the other side of the lifts and Amber was left breathless and floundering in his wake, his words not a threat so much as a promise. How had he taken the heat from her anger and directed it into another kind of heat so easily?

Damn him. He would not control her that easily. She would not let him. He might not be Cameron, but she was done with men who expected her to fall in with their wants and their demands.

When she looked up, he was holding a door open for her. 'I think I hate you,' she said as she passed to step inside the small apartment.

'Good,' he answered. 'I'm counting on it.'

It was no lie. He needed her to hate him. They could have great sex over the next few days, but if she hated him, that was all it would ever be. That was all it could ever be.

He heard the impatient tap of a cane against the floor and Mehmet, who he'd already told that he was here, was asking who he had brought along with him.

'A friend,' he said in Turkish. 'Someone I need to look after until she can join her tour group.'

Across the room, the old man smiled. 'You have never brought a friend to visit me before, Kadar.'

'She's not that kind of friend.'

'And yet still, she is here. Where is she?'

He gestured to Amber to come closer. 'He wants to meet you.'

'Me?'

'He is old,' Kadar said softly. 'Bear with him.'

'I may be blind, my young friend,' the old man said with a gappy smile, 'but I am not deaf.'

Amber crossed the small room. It was barely big enough for a few chairs around a Turkish carpet in faded colours that was probably as old as the man sitting in the chair behind, if not older. And what light there was came from the windows lining one wall. She guessed he had no need for lamps.

He was old and shrivelled and the skin on his hands resting on his chair arms resembled parchment. Around him was wrapped a robe of maroon velvet with gold trim and over his legs sat a throw, richly embroidered in shades of orange and blue with a border of stylised tulips she was already beginning to recognise as distinctly Turkish.

'Mehmet,' she said, 'my name is Amber. Amber Jones.'

His head twitched. He frowned and the lines on his face deepened. 'Amber is an unusual name,' he said, in halting, but very formal English.

'A family name,' she said.

'But you are—Australian?'

She smiled. 'My mother and her mother before her were English.'

'Come closer.' He beckoned with a crooked finger. She glanced behind her at Kadar and he sent her a look that said I told you so, and she went. Mehmet's hands reached out and she sensed that closer was not enough and that he needed to see her and so she knelt as the old man reached out craggy fingers and touched them to her head, patting her hair, finding her forehead. Old fingers. Their nails hard, their skin leathery, and yet their touch so sensitive as he skimmed her features, her forehead, the line of her jaw and chin, the pads of his fingers tracing the line of her nose and lips.

His fingers stilled, and he said something to Kadar over her head. Something she couldn't understand.

Kadar barked something back, and, although she couldn't understand the words, the meaning was plain. A denial.

Mehmet fired a response straight back and Kadar had the final word, even more emphatic this time.

She looked from one man to the other, a prickle crawling up her spine. One thing she knew for sure—they weren't talking about the weather. 'What is it?'

'It's nothing,' said Kadar. 'I told him it is your first visit to Istanbul, that is all.'

Was it all? Why would he have to point that out? She looked back to Mehmet, peered into his grizzled face. 'Mehmet?'

'Forgive an old man. It is rude to speak in a language you do not understand. Are you a thief, as Kadar says?'

'What?' Her head swung around to glare at the man standing behind her. 'No. I am not a thief.'

The old man nodded. 'I believe you. And what will you do now your tour is no more?'

'I don't know. I'm hoping to find something else.'

'Have Kadar take you to the Pavilion of the Moon. I insist.'

'I don't want to be a problem to anyone.'

The old man snorted. 'Kadar has businesses near there. It will not be a problem.'

'I'm glad you think so, old man,' Kadar said, but his voice told her he was smiling and the old man smiled and gave a wistful sigh. 'I only wish I could come with you. It has been a long time. Now, Amber Jones, give me your hand.'

Amber placed one hand upon his upturned palm on his lap, and he covered it with his other.

'Look after Kadar,' he said. 'He is a good man, but he has walked alone too long.'

'Mehmet!' he growled.

'It will not be easy, of course. He will not make it easy. You will need to be strong.'

'Mehmet,' Kadar said again, unleashing a torrent of Turkish in its wake, with not a smile in his words in sight.

'You see? I told you, he will not make it easy. Can you be strong?'

She smiled. 'I love that you care for your young friend, Mehmet, but I'm just a tourist. I can't stay. I have to go home.'

He shook his head. 'What we have to do, and what we do, sometimes they are not the same. Sometimes the way is not so clear as we think.'

'That's enough, Mehmet,' Kadar said again, his voice gruff. 'It is time for us to leave.'

'So soon? Ah, I think I have frightened off my young friend.' He gave Amber's hand a squeeze and screwed his face up with it as if deep in thought. 'Amber. Such an uncommon name, and yet, so familiar. Thank you for coming and brightening an old man's day. Come and visit me again, won't you?'

* * *

'You told him I was a thief.' Neither of them had said anything after making their farewells and they were halfway back to the apartment along grey, rain-slicked streets, both of them with hands jammed in pockets, gazing steely at the wet pavement ahead, when the niggling nagging knowledge got too much to bottle up any longer. 'Why did you tell him that?'

'Because he was talking madness. Making up stories in his head. I had to show him how wrong he was.'

'By telling him I was a thief?'

'Isn't that why the *polis* took you in?'

'I wasn't charged.'

'Only because I interceded.'

'I am not a thief.'

'And you tried to run away.'

'Only to get away from you.'

'There is no getting away from me. Not while I am responsible for your actions.'

'Look, this is pointless. There's no need to babysit me. I'm not going to get into trouble again.'

'No. Not on my watch, you're not. But where exactly did you think you were going to run to? Back to that fleapit of a hostel?'

'It wasn't that bad!'

'No?'

She grumped into silence. Okay, so maybe it wasn't that good either. And maybe she'd been crazy to think she could run away or that she even had anywhere to run away to. But she'd never been a party to the deal he'd cut with the *polis*, so that was his problem. She'd gone along with him for one night but be damned if she'd have him looking over her shoulder and watching her every move, waiting for her to transgress for the rest of her trip, whatever she ended up doing. He was too intense. Too sure of himself.

Even if he was the best lover she'd even known.

And there was another reason right there to get the hell away from him as fast as she could. Too many nights of passion like that and a girl wouldn't want to go home. A girl might start making noises about wanting to hang around. A girl might end up looking sad and getting evicted.

She didn't want to be that girl.

She wanted to draw a line under their one-night encounter and walk away, while she still could.

'I thought as much.'

Amber blinked, rewinding the conversation until she found where he was at. Still back at the hostel. Well, she'd moved on. 'I don't care what you say. It still doesn't mean I'm a thief.'

'If it is any consolation, Mehmet believes you.' He snorted. 'I think my old friend is finally losing his mind.'

'I thought he was very cogent. He's worried about you, that's all.'

'He would be better off worrying about himself.'

'So why have you never married? Is it because of your scars?'

His head snapped around. 'What is it to you?'

'You must have been very young when it happened.'

He shook his head. Maybe it would have been better for them both if he had let her run away. 'Why did you let an old man touch your face?'

The abrupt change of topic threw her. 'What?'

'To most people—most Anglophiles—having a stranger in their personal space would be foreign to them. Discomfiting at least, if not abhorrent. But you

offered your face to Mehmet's fingers without even a
trace of hesitation.'

'He's blind. How else was he expected to see me?'

'But how would you know that?'

'Maybe because it's my job to know such things.'

'Why? What do you do?'

She smiled and tossed her head back as she marched
down the street, stepping out of the way of an old
woman towing a trolley full of groceries out of a small
supermarket.

'Well?' he said, when they had come together on
the other side.

She looked across at him. 'What's it to you?'

'What?'

'Well, surely what's good for the goose is good for
the gander. Why should I tell you anything?'

He sniffed. 'It is hardly the same thing.'

'I understand you see it that way. You want to know
the answers to your questions but you don't want to give
the answers to mine.'

'That is not what I meant.'

'No. Then you meant that your questions were somehow more important than mine. Well, pardon me if I
disagree.'

'You are an infuriating woman.'

She smiled. 'Thank you.' And marched on, dodging
pedestrians, both local and tourists.

'That was not meant to be a compliment.'

'I'm taking it as one. Let me know when you've
had enough of infuriation and I'll gladly leave you in
peace.'

'You know that can't happen. Not unless a miracle
happens and your tour agency suddenly reopens.'

'Is there any chance of that?'

'That's where the miracle would come in. Until then, it appears you are stuck with me and I am stuck with you.'

'Lucky us.'

He ground his teeth together before he could answer. 'Lucky is not exactly the way I would put it.'

CHAPTER SEVEN

SHE WAS MORE than infuriating. She was exasperating. You'd think she could be grateful that she wasn't left on the streets with nowhere to go and no roof over her head. You'd think she'd show a little bit of gratitude.

Oh no.

He let her precede him into the apartment and watched the wiggle and roll of her hips as she walked past and added another adjective to describe her.

Maddening.

He must have been mad to have ever got himself involved. But those red jeans and those blue eyes and that smile that had lit up a marketplace—yes, it was a kind of madness. There was no other excuse.

And now, unless her insurance company could do something quickly—and realistically what chance of that was there when she would have to submit claims and no doubt wait weeks before she could expect any kind of pay-out?—he was stuck with her red jeans and blue eyes and electric smile.

Stuck with having her in his bed every night and waking to her every morning.

Madness.

He didn't do every night and every morning with any woman.

He watched her put her bag down and strip off her leather jacket, liking the way her sweater hugged her breasts exactly the way he wanted to.

So maybe it wasn't all bad. Last night *had* been too short, and it was only a few nights.

A few nights and he would be more than happy to let her go.

A few nights shouldn't cause any problems.

Because she was still a tourist.

She still had her return flights booked.

She was still temporary, just not as temporary as he'd first thought.

So maybe it wasn't perfect, but at least it wouldn't be a complete loss.

There was no joy for Amber when she called the travel insurance emergency line from the bedroom of Kadar's apartment. No joy at all. Only more grief.

She sat on the edge of the bed as she terminated the connection and swallowed back on an unfamiliar urge to cry. She couldn't remember the last time she'd cried. Certainly not after she'd walked in on Cameron and Chanille. She'd been too shocked and white hot with rage to cry then.

But now the prick of tears was all too close.

She'd thought the insurance company might be able to offer some emergency assistance as their policy had advertised. Maybe a little cash to go on with. Maybe even help her find an alternative tour company that might offer her credit pending her insurance claim pay-out.

Except there would be no pay-out. Because the tour company she'd booked with had lost its accreditation and was no longer recognised and therefore not covered under the terms of her insurance policy.

She should have read the small print, they'd oh, so kindly but belatedly suggested.

So she'd lost her money and there would be no pay-out.

No alternative tour.

Not even an early return home because her travel plans had been stymied.

Which meant just one thing.

Kadar wouldn't let her out of his sight until her return flights home.

Unless...

He was hanging up on his own phone call when she headed into the living room. His eyes searched her face. 'Well?'

She licked her lips and smiled weakly, thinly, knowing it was probably mad but it was a chance because it would solve all their problems. 'I don't suppose you might loan me a couple of thousand US dollars?'

He didn't so much as blink. His gaze didn't waver. 'The insurance company offered you no help?'

'The tour agency lost its accreditation six months ago.'

'So that's it?'

'Yeah, that's it. And so I thought, maybe you could loan me some money and I'll sign up for another tour. It's the low season. Someone is sure to have a space. And I could be off your hands as early as tomorrow.'

'And this is your solution?'

She shrugged. 'It would solve a lot of problems for us both. It would get me off your back and I'd see something of the Turkey I came to see.'

'When I met you, you were about to commit a criminal act. Then your tour company goes bankrupt and now you wish to borrow money from me and disappear. And if that unravels, what then? Can you see why I am not tempted by this proposition?'

'It was a mistake. An accident! And I could hardly help the tour company going broke.'

'It would be a risk for one who seems so accident prone. No, I have a better idea. You can come with me. I will show you something of Istanbul and Turkey that isn't even on the tourist trails, and you will have no need to worry about tour companies going broke or of falling foul of the authorities again. And then I will ensure you are at the airport for your flight home.'

'You'd do all that out of your overinflated sense of responsibility?

'Like I said, I take my responsibilities seriously.'

'And there's nothing in it for you?'

'I will have the company of a beautiful—if antagonistic—woman for a few days, certainly.'

'And a few nights.'

He smiled. 'As you say.'

'So this is how I am expected to pay for my private tour, then? On my back?'

'You said that, not me.'

'No, you prefer to talk about duty and pleasure. Surely it's the same thing.'

'In your mind, perhaps. I'm not going to stand here and lie and pretend that the prospect of you in my bed does not appeal. Can you be as honest? Or are you going to pretend that you did not enjoy last night's activities and you are not excited by the prospect of being naked with me again?'

'That's not the point.'

'No? What is the point, then, Amber Jones? Because all your smart little mouth is doing to me right now is making me want to shut it up and take you again, right here, right now.'

She looked in shock out of the windows, where ships and tankers dotted the Marmara Sea and if they could see out... 'It's broad daylight!'

'You make me want to get you naked and turn you to the window and together we could watch the ships glide by as I slide into you. Does that excite you?'

'You're mad,' she said, but her voice had lost its conviction because he was right. She was excited. Her senses were buzzing, her breasts were full and hard and there was an aching pulse between her thighs.

'I know. Would you like to join me in my madness?'

It must have been someone else's voice that said yes because she sure as hell didn't recognise it. It was breathy and needy and earned a growl from Kadar that rumbled through her bones.

Slowly he peeled away her clothes. Painfully slowly. Taking his time to worship whatever part of her skin he'd revealed. Her shoulders, her elbows, her breasts.

Shrugging off the shoes from her feet and peeling down the jeans from her legs and pressing his lips to the backs of her knees and her ankle and the sensitive inside of her thighs.

She trembled as he rained kisses down on her body and teased her skin with his hot tongue and the pads of his fingers, the barest heated touch to her nipples, turning the satin of her skin to goosebumps, until every part of her body screamed of one purpose and one need.

Then he turned her, and she braced herself against the window with her elbows. 'Watch the ships,' he said as his hands skimmed down her sides and over the cheeks of her behind and between, to find her wet and waiting.

He groaned and she heard the slide of a zip and the tear of a wrapper. 'Count them,' he said, his voice husky and thick.

'What?'

'Out loud. Count the ships.'

And so Amber started counting. 'One. Two. Three.' And felt the nudge of him between her thighs and at her entrance and gasped.

'Keep counting,' he said, grinding out the words.

'Four. Five.' And angled her hips. 'Six,' and felt the long hard slide of him inside until he filled her.

Words failed her, numbers failed her, her energy concentrating on trying to hold him as he slowly withdrew. She closed her eyes because she had no energy to see, only to feel.

'Count!'

'Six,' she managed as he thrust into her again, forcing her eyes wide open again. 'No. Seven. Eight.'

Oh, God!

His rhythm built. The ships moved and she lost track of which she'd counted as he moved inside her, and numbers tumbled from her lips. Numbers without rhyme or reason or an end to them because there were too many ships and remembering which number came next was too hard when all there was room for was sensation.

Nothing but sensation building upon sensation. Until he cried out behind her and with one dizzying thrust sent her hurtling, coming apart until the pieces of her shattered soul sparkled like the sun on the blue sea.

And maybe she was fickle and weak and too easily swayed by the pleasures of the flesh, but there could be worse ways to spend your days and nights, she figured as her breath steamed against the sheet of glass on her way back down to earth.

There could be much worse ways to spend your time than as a captive of Kadar.

He made good on his promise to show her Istanbul. He took her to Topkapi Palace, the old Ottoman palace, and then to Dohlmabahce Palace on the European side of the Bosphorus. She was fascinated by everything, lapping up the details and the history from the personal guides he had arranged. She oohed and aahed at the beautiful Izmir tiles of the old palace and the magnificent crystal chandeliers of the new. Like most women, she seemed fascinated by the details of the harem, but it was to the glass display cabinets that her eye was drawn and where it lingered longest.

She was like a magpie. She liked the pretty things, spending an inordinate amount of time in front of the displays, in the Treasury rooms at Topkapi Palace, and then again at Dohlmabahce, examining every coloured brooch, every jewelled scabbard and reading every typed description, a slight frown tugging her brows together.

'What are you looking for?' he asked, at one stage.

'Nothing,' she said, hastily, 'it's all just so beautiful.' He wasn't convinced by her answer. She was a woman who'd already shown herself to be partial to souvenirs and who had scant knowledge of or regard for Turkey's laws against removing antiquities. He'd like to think she wasn't so stupid as to think she could get away with spiriting anything like this home, but given how little he really knew of her and her motivations, how could he be sure? Given her interest, it was just as well everything was behind locked glass set with security alarms.

'I'm sure there are some replicas for sale in the museum shop, if you're that taken by anything.'

She gave him a tight-lipped smile. 'I'll take a look.'

It took hours to wend their way through the two palaces, so that the evening was already gathering, rain showers sending up the dark umbrellas, the street lighting sending ribbons of colour along the damp grey streets.

For Kadar and Amber, there was no lining up for tour buses to take them back to their hotels. Kadar's driver arrived with his car to whisk them away no more than a moment after they'd emerged from the gates of the palace.

But while Amber's feet were ready to fall off by the time they were through, and she'd never been more grateful than for a private car ride back to Kadar's apartment, her mind was in overdrive.

For her great-great-great-grandmother had turned twenty and left home on her adventures in eighteen fifty-six, the same year Dohlmabahce Palace had been completed, before she had seemingly disappeared off the face of the earth for five years.

What had happened to her all those missing years in a foreign country so far from home? Had she wandered the rooms of the harem as her hushed family lore liked to hint? And had her eyes witnessed any of the wonders that her descendant of five generations had witnessed today?

It was intoxicating to imagine they had. A century and a half meant nothing in the scope of such historic places.

'You seem deep in thought.'

She looked over at him and found a smile. She might

be stuck with him, but he really was trying to make up for her lost tour. 'It was a fabulous day, thank you.'

'You appeared to be very taken by the jewels.'

The warm bubble of gratefulness she'd been feeling burst right then and there. There was something unsaid in his words that she didn't like. A warning.

But then, it was the jewellery that had been niggling at her. And her bracelet in particular. She'd never seen jewellery or treasures that reminded her so much of the style of her bracelet. She'd imagined it must be cheap, because it featured so many different colours all together in the one piece. But so much of what she'd seen today was strikingly similar. Different coloured gems sitting alongside each other, all of them beautiful in their own right, but together an ostentatious display of wealth.

It still didn't mean it wasn't a cheap replica Amber had bought in a market at the time though, just that she had been jolted by the similarity in design.

And really, the more she thought about it, the more it made sense that it was an early knock off. It was too ridiculous for words to think that something genuine could have been sitting wrapped in oilskins along with what was left of Amber's diary, in her gran's attic in a tiny hamlet in rural Hertfordshire for so many years.

'Well,' she said, 'who wouldn't be impressed? It was a spectacular display.'

'It was. Turkey is very proud of its heritage.'

Another message. Another thinly veiled warning? She was sure of it.

And for a moment she toyed with the idea of telling him about her intrepid forebear, whose diary and bracelet she'd found, and who'd ventured to Turkey all those years ago, inspired by the adventures of trail-blazing women like Jane Digby who'd gone before in following their heart rather than settling into the constraints and expectations of English society.

But would he even believe her? Doubtful, given the way he appeared too willing to want to believe the worst of her.

He already thought she was a thief. If she told him now about the bracelet, and it did turn out to be anything other than a cheap copy, then he'd only ask where she'd stolen it from. And given it was old, even if it was a cheap copy back then, it was bound to be worth something now, even as a collector's item.

She might as well save herself the grief.

Besides, why should she bare her all when he had his own secrets? He already knew more about her than most people did, courtesy of of the fact he'd been there when she'd been interviewed by the *polis*. But what did she really know about him? Nothing. So why should she tell him any more about herself?

So she simply said, 'Turkey has every right to be proud of its heritage.' And smiled. Let him build a case against her out of that.

And when he'd turned, stony faced, away, as if she hadn't given him what he'd been hoping for, she asked the question she'd been meaning to ever since their visit to the old man and had forgotten in the excitement of today's adventures. 'Tell me about Mehmet.'

His head swung back around. 'What about him?'

'Who is he?'

'An old friend. Why?'

'Just curious. How old is he, do you know?'

Alongside her Kadar shrugged. 'At least, ninety. Probably closer to ninety-five.'

'How do you know him? Through your family?'

He looked out of his window. 'No.'

'Then—'

He turned back. 'What is this?'

'I'm just making conversation. What was the Pavilion of the Moon he mentioned? I haven't read about that anywhere.'

'You're not making conversation. You're prying.'

'So, I'm curious. Or is being curious a crime here, too?'

He gave an impatient flick of his head and she pushed herself deeper into the plush leather of her seat. He could keep his damned secrets if they were that special. She turned her attention out of the window and watched the late afternoon traffic jostling for position on the busy highway, the coloured street lights making patterns on the slick roads.

'You heard today about the sultans and the harem of the Ottoman empire.'

She looked around, surprised. 'Yes.'

'When the empire came to an end in the early twentieth century, and the Sultan exiled, palace life, as it had been for centuries, came to an end. The women and the men were freed from service.

'Mehmet's mother was one of the women of the palace, from the harem. His adopted father, one of the Sultan's vizier's. His many years of service meant he could buy a house and they set up home together, two displaced souls in a world that had moved on. In addition, there was a small palace he had been gifted for his faithful service previously.'

'The Pavilion of the Moon.'

Kadar nodded and stretched out his arm along the back of the seat, his fingers draping over her shoulder, his thumb making lazy sweeps of her arm. She was sure he had not a clue he was doing it. 'It was a folly constructed by an earlier sultan, some say as an escape from the hothouse atmosphere of palace life here. A place to be more normal.' He shrugged. 'Of course, a sultan could never live a normal life. It is Mehmet's to use until his death, though it was always to be returned to the state. Already there are steps under way to turn it into a museum, and then you will see it listed on your tourist trails.'

Amber wondered. Mehmet was more than just an old man. He was a link joining the present to the past. But something niggled.

'You said Mehmet's father adopted him?'

'Yes. He was already an old man when the empire crumbled, but he could not have had children of his own anyway. He was a eunuch, of course.'

'Oh.'

His fingers stilled. 'Does that shock you?'

'No. It's just—' There was a flip side to the jewels and the rich costumes and a lifestyle of luxury and indulgence, Amber realised, a flip side to chandeliers and staircases made all of crystal, to the gilt ceilings and the romanticism of what life in the palace must have been like. And it was the stark truth that the Sultan and what was his had to be protected, and by men who could be trusted.

And she thought about Kadar, masculine and virile, and shuddered when she thought what a waste of a man that would be. 'It just seems so cruel.'

'Life can be cruel. But he led a good life—pampered, many would say, and then he lived out his life with the woman he took as his wife and brought Mehmet up as his own son.'

As Mehmet had done with him, Kadar thought uneasily. Paying it forward. Giving a child a father when he had none. A semblance of family where his had been cruelly ripped away.

A lump formed in the back of his throat.

He owed the old man everything. But he already knew that. He didn't have to tell this woman about him to appreciate how much the old man had done for him.

Maddening.

That was what she was.

They ate that night at a restaurant near the fish markets of Kumkapi on the Sea of Marmara, where the fish were displayed in patterns on trays like works of art, and where locals and tourists alike mixed to enjoy the atmosphere and the freshest catches from the sea, and afterwards they made love long into the night.

And the next day he escorted her around the Grand Bazaar before he surprised her by taking her on the Bosphorus cruise she'd missed.

Amber was beyond excited. The day was mostly clear, and seeing Istanbul from the water gave the city another dimension. They sat on the deck of the boat protected from the breeze and with the thin winter sun shining down on them and cruised down the waterway that separated two continents, sea birds wheeling behind them, hoping to be thrown a crust of bread.

They sailed past palaces and ancient fortresses, apartment buildings marching up the sides of the hills and quaint timber houses alike. A huge container ship heading from the Black Sea passed them by as they sailed under the Bosphorus bridge that joined Europe to Asia within the one country.

And as Amber swivelled her camera to capture the

views it seemed Istanbul only became more remarkable and more beautiful.

Kadar watched her as she took photos of the bridge, the castle, the Turkish flag flapping proudly in the bow of the boat with the white wake spilling behind, her enthusiasm infectious, and, for all her faults, she reminded him of all that was good about his adopted homeland. She reminded him of all the things he'd once marvelled at and somehow forgotten in his acceptance of this place as his home.

It was good to see Istanbul from a visitor's point of view.

And he looked at her once again, with the ends of her hair whipping around her face and her bright blue eyes smiling and her smile so wide, and he thought, no. More than that. It was good to see Istanbul from this woman's point of view. She made Istanbul shiny and exciting and new. She made everything she saw a discovery. A delight.

And it was no hardship to be seen with her. He saw the glances from other men on the boat. The looks of envy. The wishing.

But more than that.

For despite the fact this was an obligation he'd accepted, it was simply no hardship to be with her.

He'd never spent much time with any woman. Had never felt the need or the compunction. But now he was obliged to spend his days with this woman, it was some relief that he didn't feel as if it would be a chore seeing out his obligations.

Establishing some kind of rapport during the day would make their time together much more bearable.

Would make their nights together more workable.

That was all.

That *was* all.

Because even when he could hear his friends Zoltan and Bahir joking and asking who would be next to be married, there was no fear of that. Because this wasn't about marriage.

This was about duty. Nothing more. And there was no risk, he told himself, because she was still going home at the end of it.

Seven more nights and she would be gone.

Which gave him seven more nights to enjoy her pleasures before she got on that plane and disappeared for ever.

He wasn't about to waste a single one of them.

'Thank you,' she said, with an unexpected kiss to his cheek as the boat docked back at its berth.

'What for?' he asked as they waited for the gangway to be organised. 'It was only the tour that you were going to take.'

'I know. But I thought I'd missed my chance. But that was so special, thank you.'

Her face was open. Honest. Without a hint of artifice, her blue eyes sparkling bright, her lips turned into a wide smile. And it struck him that maybe he'd been too hard on her. Maybe he'd been wrong.

Mehmet had believed her and he might be blind but he was nobody's fool.

No. He shook his thoughts free of that uncomfortable thought as she stepped up onto the gangplank. She'd been caught in the act. He'd witnessed it, not Mehmet. And he'd seen the way her eyes were drawn to Turkey's treasures. Just because she was beautiful it did not equate with innocent, in anyone's language.

'Where are we going next?' she asked as he handed

her off the boat, and onto the dock. 'Or have you had
enough of playing tour guide?'

There were so many more places Kadar could have
shown her, but the way the loose ends of her hair played
about her face in the breeze reminded her of the one
place he knew he had to take her. A place of mystery
and atmosphere that she should not miss.

'Come,' he said, mysteriously. 'I will show you.'

CHAPTER EIGHT

IT WAS ONLY a short walk to the small, unassuming building that sat atop one of Istanbul's ancient wonders.

'The Basilica Cistern,' she said as he bought tickets. 'I read something about this, but I didn't realise it was right here. We walked past it on the way from the *polis* station and I had no idea.'

'So what did you read?'

'That it was some kind of ancient water storage.'

He nodded and they went inside, and what Amber saw took her breath away. 'Oh, my God,' she whispered. 'It's enormous.' And it was. As impressive as a cathedral, with its soaring arched roof and row upon row of columns, softly lit from below with spotlights that turned the interior of the vast space golden.

It was cool down here, and quiet, the sounds of the city so close above muted by thick brickwork, the only sounds the murmur of tourists, the sound of piped music and the constant drip drip of water from the ceiling into the pool below.

They climbed down the steps to the timber walkway built between the columns, huge carp and goldfish swimming in the water below.

She had a pamphlet to tell her the details, but it was Kadar who filled in the history, his rich deep voice adding to the hypnotic quality of the atmosphere. He told her of its construction back in the sixth century, the columns recycled from other sites, one column turned green with algae from the constant slide of water and decorated in the peacock eyes and tears, said to represent tears for the many slaves who died in the cistern's construction.

And if she'd thought Kadar's aura would be dwarfed by such a magnificent construction, she'd have been wrong. He seemed to charge the air with his presence, turning an eerie space electric with excitement and mystery and danger.

He didn't touch her, but she was more aware of him than ever. She could feel him through the damp air at the back of her neck. Feel his dark eyes watching her from behind. Her skin prickled, and she had never been more grateful for the presence of other tourists. It was winter and there were only a few, mostly couples spread around the walkways, their voices hushed or silent as they listened to audio tours and took photo after photo, but if she'd been alone down here with just this man... she would not trust him. She would not trust herself.

They would make love after this.

She knew it. She felt it in the pull between their bodies and the vibrations in the air between them.

And maybe this time it would be different.

Maybe this time he might let her take the lead.

No, not maybe.

She would make it so.

They followed the walkway and made their way deeper into the cistern, the fish darting this way and that in the waters beneath. 'Here,' he said. 'This is what I want you to see.'

She blinked. Another column, with a walkway all around, and she could understand why, because the heavy base rested on a stone face, set sideways against the floor.

'Is it a woman?' she asked him.

'Medusa,' he said, and Amber realised it was not braids around her face, but snakes. 'Who could turn a man to stone with one look. She and her twin were taken from a building somewhere and transplanted here.'

'Her twin?'

Of course, there was another, this time the head set upside down beneath the column.

'Why?' she asked.

'Nobody knows for sure. Some say to negate the power of the gorgon's gaze. Some say to protect the building by warding off evil spirits.'

The cistern had been full once, an underground reservoir of water brought from many kilometres away via aqueduct to supply the Topkapi Palace and surrounding city, where now just a few feet remained, and it was bizarre to think all this, the Medusas' heads and the column of peacock eyes and tears, had been underwater, hidden away for centuries and then lost for many more when the cistern was forgotten for a time.

She shivered, as if an evil spirit had brushed past her shoulder, a warning, cold and malevolent. And then she turned her gaze to Kadar and the raw desire in his eyes vanquished any thoughts of evil and filled the space where it had been with a heated promise until her body hummed with expectation.

Around her the columns glowed, silent sentinels, rich with the history of the ages, as the flute music from the speakers floated in the air between, haunting and melodic, the drip, drip of water gently echoing in the high-ceilinged space. 'Thank you for showing me this. It's beautiful,' she said.

He touched a hand to her hair, unravelling from the knot she'd tied it in this morning long before their cruise and the sea breeze that had toiled so hard to tug it undone. 'You made me think of Medusa,' he said, his touch so electric, her breath jagged in her throat. 'The way your hair floats around your face.'

'Be careful,' she warned, trying to defuse the moment, because in this moment he was so intense, his body almost vibrating with tension before her. 'Or I might turn you to stone.'

His mouth kicked up at one corner. 'You already have.'

The shudder that followed his admission turned her knees weak. She turned away, needing to grab onto the boardwalk's balustrade for support, momentarily thrown by the his electric words and the power he was giving her. Surely mere lust wasn't supposed to make your chest tight or make you feel this emotionally charged?

She felt his breath then, soft and warm upon her neck, felt him behind her the way she was finding he liked, felt his impatience, and knew that if they'd been alone he'd have taken her here and now over the balustrade amongst the forest of golden columns and the secrets of the past.

Her breath hitched, as she knew her body would welcome it. 'I think I've seen enough.'

'In that case,' he said, his voice gruff and strained, and taking her arm as he led her towards the exit, 'we should go.'

He wasted no time calling for his car. He wasn't about to waste time walking.

Not when all he wanted was to bury himself deep inside this woman.

He no sooner had her inside the apartment than he was pulling her into his arms, his mouth hard against hers. Hungry. Impatient. Wanting.

She came willingly, hot and ready, as he'd known she would be. She pushed his coat from his shoulders as he peeled away her jacket. They fought like that, mouths locked together, grappling with garments in their rush to be naked, discarding pieces of clothing in a trail across the floor as they headed inexorably towards the bedroom. Her jeans, his trousers, shucked off, everything abandoned.

And when he got her to the bed, he sat her on the edge, his hands sliding the lace boy leg underwear down her legs as his mouth feasted upon hers, in such a hurry that he almost forgot about protection—again—before he swiped it up.

She took it from him and he let her, breath hissing through his teeth as she held it at his tip with one hand and rolled it down his long hard length with the other. It was by grinding his teeth that he could hold himself together, the mere seconds it took her nimble fingers feeling like for ever.

But finally she was done and he took her hands and he kissed her again where she still sat on the edge of the bed. Kissed her until she was liquid and pliant against his hot mouth.

She leaned back, trying to draw him down on the bed over her.

And he was ready.

He made to flip her over onto her stomach.

She resisted.

And he wanted to be inside her and inside her now

but she was tugging on his arms as she fell back onto the bed, pulling him down on top of her.

'This way,' she said, angling her hips in encouragement.

'No,' he said, and shrugged off her hands, pushing himself to his feet. 'What are you playing at? Roll over.'

'Why?'

'It is better.'

'For who?'

'For everyone.'

'No. I want you this way. I want to see you this time.'

'No!'

'Why?'

'Are you mad? Why do you think?' He turned then, exposing the full horror of his scars to her again. 'Do you imagine for one second that you want your hands on this mess? Do you think I want your hands anywhere near it? To feel your revulsion when your fingers connect with this?'

She sat up, crossed her legs, her hands resting demurely on her lap, and if she hadn't been sitting naked with her hair tousled on the edge of his bed, she could almost have been applying for a job. 'Fine. So I won't touch you there.'

He growled with frustration. 'Why can't we just do this my way?'

'Why can't we try it my way? I'll hold on to the coverlet with my hands. Even better, handcuff me to the bed head. You might enjoy that.'

'Don't be ridiculous. This is not a joke!'

'I'm not joking! But I don't want to count ships and I don't want to look at any more bathroom tiles and I certainly don't want to have to stare at a coverlet on a bed. I want to see you. I want to feel your body on top of mine.'

'You can.'

'Not the way you want. I am neither a horse nor a dog to be mounted like an animal!' She laid one hand on her breast, another on her belly. 'I want to feel you here, and here, against me.'

He shook his head. It wouldn't work. It couldn't. Sooner or later she would forget and her hands would touch him and she would flinch or worse, and he would feel her revulsion and disgust.

It would happen, he knew.

But seeing her touch herself stirred something inside him. Thinking about tying her hands down stirred him even more. He wasn't in the habit of restraining his women. But then, until now, he'd never had need. His women were temporary and he called the shots. Nobody had ever suggested—*offered*—to be restrained. 'I don't have any handcuffs.'

Her eyes sparked. 'Use a belt. A tie.' She held out her hands wrists together for him. 'I promise, I'll go quietly.'

He took the space of a heartbeat to decide, before swiping a tie from the rack inside his wardrobe door. 'I promise,' he said as he lashed her proffered wrists together, 'you won't come the same way.'

She shunted up the bed and he tied her hands to the bed post, her arms over her head, and then he rocked back, drinking in the picture she made. Her arms pulled her breasts high, stretching skin over her ribcage, accentuating the dip to her waist and the soft curve of her belly, cradled within the twin jut of her hipbones.

And he wondered that this had never occurred to him, not that any woman would have looked as good as this woman did right here. Right now.

His prisoner.

He growled, low in his throat, his cock bucking. Aching. He grabbed her ankles and pushed her legs apart, sliding his hands up her legs as he followed their progress on his knees.

He liked this idea more and more. He could take his pleasure this way. He could take her any way he liked. He could feast on her with his mouth. He could torture her slowly until she begged for release.

Next time.

This time he wasn't planning on taking that long.

He took his own sweet time joining her, but the look in his eyes told her he liked it. A lot.

She felt excited and exposed, and for the first time she felt a frisson of fear.

What had made her brave enough to suggest something she'd never tried? She didn't know this man, not really, so why should she trust him? Why would she put herself into a position where she was completely at his mercy?

But that knowledge only ramped up her excitement.

Her nipples ached, bolt-hard as his searing gaze scorched a heated trail over her skin.

He touched her, testing her, and breath hissed through her teeth. He smiled, his fingertips sliding over slick, ultra-sensitive flesh.

'What do you want?'

'You,' she said, with more breath than voice. 'Inside me. So stop messing me around.'

His smile widened.

'You are bold, for one who is tied. And given you are my captive, and so desperate, I could so easily just walk away and torture you some more.'

She bucked against her bound wrists and said, 'Don't you damn well dare walk away now!'

And he laughed. God, she made him laugh, even when he was already aching for her.

'Then perhaps, instead,' he said, 'I might choose to be merciful.'

He positioned himself between her thighs and leaned over and took one nipple in his mouth, grazing it with his teeth, laving it with his tongue. First one and then the other, before sliding his hand behind her head and claiming her mouth, his hot tongue tangling with hers. Her nipples brushed against his chest and her back arched, seeking more. Because yes, this was what she'd craved. Feeling his chest against hers. Making love face to face.

She tugged at her wrists, straining against her bonds, wanting to pull him to her, needing to be free, but her bonds held. And then she needed something else more, and he gave it to her, in one long, heart-stopping thrust that drove her head back against her pillow, and that made her forgot about her bound wrists because it was a different kind of freedom her body now craved.

For every thrust, every evocative slide of flesh against flesh took her closer to that place. Feeling his legs nestled between her thighs. Feeling the driving surge of his hips. Feeling his hot breath against her throat as he dropped to his elbows to surge into her.

There was nowhere to go but with him.

In the end, there was nowhere to go but everywhere.

Her release came gift-wrapped in a scream and with Kadar's name etched into the ribbon that tied it into a bow, and from the depths of beyond she thought she heard someone crying out her name, and that was the greatest gift of all.

It took a long time for her body to pull the fragmented pieces of itself together, and to hum down from that amazing place.

But then, it was bound to take a while.

Because he was an amazing lover. He was a magician at the love arts. He could conjure an orgasm from thin air with one heated look and the press of a fingertip.

No doubt even less.

And she could understand why he'd want to make love with her in a way her hands couldn't reach around to touch his back and remind him of his scars.

She could understand completely.

But she should have let him keep making love to her that way. She should never have insisted on him making love to her face to face.

Because she'd just lost a tiny seed of resentment against him, right there, and instead found a whole new reason to wish he might keep on making love to her.

And she could do with a reason to resent him, if she was to think about going home.

But how could she forget that this was Kadar, who'd already branded her a thief and was happy to tell others the same? She didn't need to look for reasons to resent him. How could she forgive him that?

She dragged in air, her body slowly spinning, coming down from the dizzy heights he'd taken her to. She couldn't. But still, right at this moment, feeling boneless and replete, the only resentment she felt was that her time with Kadar was already ticking down.

A fact that should not make her feel half as sorry as it did.

CHAPTER NINE

MORE THAN ONE thousand kilometres from Istanbul's busy streets, the town of Burguk could have been on another planet. The valley in which the town nestled ringed with mountains topped with snow while the landscape was lunar, rocks the colour of sand, carved into strange shapes by the weather.

The stone buildings of the town hunkered into the land as if the wind had carved them out too, as if they were part of the landscape. As if they belonged.

It was a harsh landscape, but with a kind of stark beauty that drew the eye. Snow had filled the streets the week before and promised to again before too long, but for now the melting snow was piled in dirty heaps on the roadsides and skinny trees pointed bare branches towards the sky, as if begging for warmth from the thin sun.

'It's beautiful,' she said as their car topped a rise that gave them a view over the entire valley and Kadar asked their driver to pull over.

The wind whipped and tugged at her hair and at the hem of his cashmere coat as they walked to the edge of the ridge overlooking the valley, set out before them like a shallow, wide basin edged in low hills and ringed with snow-topped mountains. The wind could be nothing but icy cold.

'It's not dissimilar to Cappadocia,' he said, 'just not on so grand a scale.'

'My tour was supposed to spend two days there.'

'I am sorry you were forced to miss some of the places your tour was supposed to cover.'

She wasn't. Not now. It wasn't as if she couldn't come back some time, find a tour agency that was accredited and reputable and visit the places she'd missed. Besides, if her tour agency hadn't folded, she wouldn't be here now, in this man's presence, discovering a part of Turkey that she'd never known existed.

Hell, she wouldn't be here with this man, period. And to think she'd once resented his insistence that he watch over her.

How could she be sorry when her days were filled with adventure and her nights were filled with the discoveries of the flesh?

Something had changed last night, when he'd made love to her face to face. Something had subtly shifted in the balance between them.

And that change left her feeling as uncomfortable as it had left her gratified.

'I'll come back one day,' she said, shrugging her shoulders against the cold wind and the icy fingers trying to find their way under her scarf. 'All those sights have been there centuries. They'll all still be there.'

'Maybe you will come back for your honeymoon.'

She looked across at him. Had he been tapping into her thoughts? Was he warning her not to think this was anything more than temporary? He should have kept listening and then he'd have got to the part about never falling for a man who couldn't trust you implicitly, even if the sex was mind-blowing. That might have given him a measure of comfort.

But until then, she might as well play along.

'What a great idea,' she said. 'Maybe I will. And I'll be sure to bring him around to meet you, don't worry.'

'That would not be such a good idea.' But there was a smile behind his words that told her he knew she was kidding.

He ushered her back towards the car, wondering at this woman who didn't quake in fear or even take him seriously but bounced shots right back at him. He'd smiled, even though her words grated on him. There was no place for her in his future—even as a visitor. There was even less place for a partner. He didn't want to think of another man with her, then or now. Which was a thought that gave him pause. Because he'd never asked...

'Do you have a boyfriend back in Australia?'

She stopped halfway back to the car and turned to him. 'That seems a very odd question to ask someone after the things we've done together.'

He shrugged. 'Do you?'

She searched his eyes, and sighed, looking for the message in his words, when he'd already made it plain that this was temporary. 'You have already branded me a thief. And now, I see, you're attributing me with the morals of an alley cat. If you want me to be impatient for being free of you, you're going the right way about it.' She turned to walk away and he stopped her with his hand on her arm.

'I am surprised if you do not, that is all. I was not trying to insult you.'

'You could have fooled me. If your woman was travelling in another country, how would you feel if she slept with another man while she was there?'

'It would not happen. She would not be my woman if she could do such a thing.'

'Then why would you possibly imagine I could do that? Unless you thought I was some kind of tart.'

'I have already told you, I didn't mean that. I just do not understand why a woman such as you wouldn't have a man.'

'You mean a thief like me?'

'I mean beautiful like you.'

She closed her eyes, swallowing against a shudder. She wished he hadn't said that. It was pointless. Irrelevant. And dulled the edges of her resentment and made her wish that he was another man because she could not afford to go falling for this one.

'I had a man, as it happens. Though more a worm than a man, come to think of it.'

Dark brows drew together. 'What happened?'

'I found him in bed with my best friend.' She gave a tight smile. 'Not my favourite day, that one.'

He stood there, dark eyes meeting blue as the cold wind whipped around them both, and she held her breath, praying that he didn't say he was sorry. She couldn't bear it if he pitied her.

'He was a fool.'

She breathed out again, relieved. 'Perhaps.' And while it had been nice to hear Kadar's assessment equated with her own, it hadn't been Cameron who'd been the biggest fool. 'I'm well rid of him and I'm not looking to go down that particular route again any time soon, so, you see, you have nothing to fear from me.'

'I had nothing to fear from you anyway.'

She smiled, but it was half through gritted teeth this time, and she wondered at a conversation that seemed to have more twists and turns than a grand prix track.

'Other than I might sneak off with the silverware, you mean.'

'No, it is you who needs to fear, if that happens.'

She blinked. 'I'll keep that in mind.'

'That would be wise.'

A few kilometres beyond the town, they pulled up outside a high stone wall. 'Welcome to the Pavilion of the Moon,' Kadar said as their driver took care of their luggage.

Amber was confused. All she could see behind the wall was a cliff face, soaring high. Until he swung the gate open and she could see the tall timber doors and the windows, set into the cliff itself.

She imagined it must be tiny, one or two rooms at most, so she was in no way prepared for the sheer magnitude of it when he opened the heavy doors. It was a miniature palace that had been dug out under the cliff, with columns and archways carved from the stone, and arched alcoves cut into the walls that contained richly decorated vases and urns. Silk rugs lay scattered on the floor and dark timber furniture contrasted against walls that subtly placed lamps turned golden.

'It's incredible,' she said, turning full circle to take it all in. 'And a sultan stayed here?'

'On occasion. It was a long journey from the city then called Constantinople, but yes, this was his retreat.'

'Who would have thought of it?'

'There were caves in the cliffs that shepherds used over the centuries. They'd been abandoned when the Sultan's hunting party camped here under the moon and found them.'

'It's fabulous.'

He smiled. 'There is more.' Her enthusiasm was infectious, the spat they'd had at the ridge top clearly forgotten in her excitement.

He showed her through the many rooms, leaving the Sultan's suite one of the last, anticipating her delight, not disappointed when her eyes lit up. She brightened up anywhere that she smiled.

The room was palatial, the posts of the bed actual columns carved from the stone, archways leading to an expansive bathroom complete with a heated slab of stone for the *hamam* and a sunken bath. Marble tiles lined the walls and floor and there were feature tiles with tulips, a splash of red and green to break up the gold of marble and walls.

'Do you think you will be happy here for a few days while I take care of business?'

She turned those lapis lazuli eyes at him and shook her head. 'How could I not? I can't believe how lucky I am to actually stay here. It's magnificent.'

And because those eyes shone like gems, he could not help himself. 'I'm sorry,' he said.

A frown tugged at her brows. 'What for?'

'For our little disagreement before. I am not used to having a woman around.' Not for longer than the time it took to bed her, that was. 'I am used to being on my own.'

'I'm sorry you got lumbered with me.'

He was about to say he was sorry too. Except he wasn't. Not any more. Now he looked for her wonder and her smiles, and every one of them lit up his solitary life just a little bit more.

It was good to have her around. Just for a while.

Not that he would tell her any of that.

'We all have to do our duty,' he said stiffly as he led her back into the bedroom. 'There are other rooms to show you, but you must excuse me, I am expected elsewhere.'

'What is this mysterious business of yours that brings you all the way out here?'

'It's no mystery. I have a factory here.'

'That makes what?'

'Pyrotechnics.'

'You make fireworks?'

'Yes. And run a business that organises displays all over the world, amongst other things.'

'But isn't that dangerous?'

He glanced at her. 'It can be.'

She was distracted from asking more questions when she saw their bags sitting inside the door of the Sultan's bedroom.

'Why is our luggage here?'

'Where else did you think we were going to sleep?'

'But it's the Sultan's room.'

'You would prefer not to sleep in the Sultan's bed?'

'I didn't think it would be allowed.'

'When the Pavilion of the Moon is turned into a museum, it will not be. But for now, it belongs to Mehmet and he has offered us his hospitality. It would be churlish to refuse.'

She thought about that, and what an amazing gift she'd been given when Mehmet had offered the use of the Pavilion of the Moon during their stay.

'I'd hate to be seen as churlish.'

He smiled and kissed her lightly on the lips. 'Then it is decided.'

Amber chose to be dropped in town to explore on foot, while Kadar attended his meetings. There weren't many tourists and she drew plenty of curiosity with her blond hair and blue eyes as she wandered from shop to shop.

She wasn't worried about being by herself. Kadar had assured her she would be safe. Everyone knew, he said, that she was with him. How he could be so certain, she didn't know.

But besides, she wasn't really alone. A small boy had taken to following her, shadowing her a few steps back, and looking around ingenuously whenever she happened to catch sight of him behind her.

He made her smile and she was happy to let him drift along behind her, trying to pretend he wasn't there.

She found a handicrafts shop, selling local crafts, and she noticed an embroidered throw in the window like the one she'd seen around Mehmet's legs. Like his, it had a border of stylised tulips surrounding a richly coloured pattern of shapes and crooked trees. Her mother would love it. And now that Kadar had so generously picked up all her expenses, she knew her money would last and she could afford to buy a few souvenirs for her family.

Five minutes later she emerged from the shop with the throw in a gift bag, surprised at the price the man in the shop had charged, but he'd insisted the ridiculously tiny amount was correct. She would check with Kadar later but for some reason she felt she'd been given a huge discount. So she very happily bought an evil eye keyring for her brother and a coffee table book of Turkish landscape photographs for her father into the deal.

She smiled and said hello when she saw her shadow waiting patiently for her outside, but he just looked around as if he didn't know who she was talking to.

She bought a simple cup of pomegranate juice from a man with a cart who sliced the fat red fruit and spun a lever to press the fruit juice and let the juice run free. And when she tried to pay him, he waved the payment away. 'Please,' she insisted, pointing to a painted sign that clearly displayed the price in Turkish lire, but he insisted.

So instead she held out the money for the small boy who was waiting a little distance away. He blinked at her uncertainly and so she nodded and he grinned and came running up, laughing when he held the coins in his hand.

He ran off shouting and she looked up to see the man at the juice cart smiling widely himself.

She shrugged and wandered away, sipping on the red juice, both sweet and tart and refreshing, when she heard a commotion behind her and she turned and saw a group of children running, headed by the boy she'd given the few coins to. She caught the eye of the juice cart man who was laughing and it was his turn to shrug as the children surrounded her,

'Okay,' she said, 'you can have lire too, but give me a guided tour around the town first.'

Between her clumsy hand signals and the assistance of the juice seller, the children shouted their agreement, shepherding her around the sights of the town, past the baker's shop, and the spice shop that sold sweets and fruit and the school where they went. All the sights that were important to them. And as they went her little group of tour guides grew.

She loved it, as amused by them as they were by her, until she found a small girl trailing behind them, a small girl who walked with a limp, and a lump came to her throat as she was reminded of her tiny cousin, Tash, born with more problems than any child deserved, and how still she'd seemed to have a heart as big as a lion as she'd struggled to keep up with big sisters and her cousins as they'd played. Although as it turned out, her heart had never been that big or that strong...

She swallowed.

Amber had been fifteen years old when Tash's frail body had given up.

And for the first time, Amber felt a little homesick, missing her class of children at the school where she worked in Melbourne's suburbs, and their unconditional love and hugs. On an impulse, she scooped the blinking child up into her arms and carried her the rest of the way.

When Kadar found her, she was sitting in a café near a brazier peeling oranges for a clutch of children, a little girl sitting in her lap, busily watching Amber's nimble fingers work. An orange in her own hands, she was trying to copy her movements. And he was surprised, despite the various reports he'd been hearing.

'I heard we had a new pied piper in the town.' She looked up, blinking, before she grinned. The little girl in her lap looked up at him, her eyes wide. He smiled at the scene before him. 'Had a good afternoon with your new friends?'

'The best. Who told you?'

'Just about everyone I spoke to. News travels fast here. You're quite a hit with the locals.'

Her eyes narrowed. 'I suspect that may have something to do with you. Everywhere I went, I seemed to score a bargain. Even the bag of oranges—surely they must have been flown in this time of year?'

Kadar shrugged and gave nothing away as silently the children watched them, their expressions uncertain as the adults spoke in a language they understood only a word or two of as yet. Until he said something to them and they nodded and smiled and ran away, pieces of orange clutched in their hands. The little girl in her lap gave Amber a hug and clambered down. She had a twisted leg, Kadar realised, as he watched her hobble away, trying to catch up with the others, the orange Amber she'd been working on held precious to her chest.

'Does she have far to go?' she asked, watching the child, and he realised she actually cared. And it shouldn't matter, but somehow it registered in a place he wasn't used to going.

'No,' he said, his voice sounding as if it had been poured over gravel, even to him. 'Nothing is far here.' But he wondered all the same.

'I like Burguk,' she said, using napkins to soak up the juice from her hands. 'I like the people here. I like the children.'

'I told them they would see you tomorrow,' he said. 'At the feast the village is preparing.'

She brushed her jeans off as she stood to collect her things together. 'In honour of your visit, you mean?'

He shrugged. 'It has been a good year. It is an occasional custom.'

She shook her head as she collected up her shopping. 'Who are you?' she asked. 'I thought you were just a businessman. But the people here seem to love you.'

'Who are you?' he countered. 'I thought you would spend your time in Burguk idly shopping, but then I find you have wooed the entire village.'

Her smile widened as he offered her his hand and she filled it with the handles of her bags. 'I shopped, don't worry.'

Amber lay on the Sultan's bed, her body slick with sweat as she panted her way down from the dizzy heights Kadar had taken her to.

Above the bed the constellations had been reproduced so that it seemed as if they were lying under the desert sky, the stars tiny pinpricks of light.

Amber wanted to pinch herself. She'd come to Turkey in the hopes of getting a taste of the country her great-great-great-grandmother had so clearly loved, never expecting that she'd find her own adventure.

Would have pinched herself, if she'd been able to use her hands.

'Um, I hate to bother you, but…'

Kadar lifted his head from where he'd buried it against her neck when he'd collapsed against her, his brow drawn into a frown that lasted only as long as it took her to tug on her bindings, and his frown disappeared and turned into a smile.

'You have a problem?'

'Only if you don't untie me.'

His smile grew wider and made her toes curl and her mind send an alert to be careful. A playful Kadar was a dangerous beast. A playful Kadar made her wish things that were playful might be more permanent. And that was a dangerous place to be.

'I don't know why I didn't think of it before—the perfect way to keep you out of trouble.'

'You'll be in trouble if you don't untie me.'

'No sense of humour,' he joked as he kissed her cheek and reached up to untie her hands. His skin smelt of sweat and sex and hot-blooded man and she breathed him in, wanting to imprint it on her mind so she would never forget.

She rubbed her wrists as she brought her arms down and he captured them in his hand and kissed the insides of her wrists. 'Does that hurt?'

'Not really,' she said, though she'd tugged hard against

her restraints, because it was worth a little pain to feel this man between her legs and feel his chest against her breasts and his mouth upon her lips.

A little pain was so worth it.

CHAPTER TEN

THERE WAS A holiday mood in the village the next day and it seemed as if the entire valley was celebrating, all the people of the small villages and towns coming together to celebrate a good year.

They gathered at the local football ground, setting up food stalls and braziers to ward off the chill, a colder night forecast because the snow clouds had scudded away and left the sky clear. Big spits roasted whole sheep turning the air mouth-watering. Amber recognised the man she'd bought the pomegranate juice from the day before and the man who'd sold her the souvenirs, both excited to meet her again and introduce her to their wives and families. And the children who'd shown her around the town brought their parents to meet her. Half the town seemed eager to meet her.

She was charmed by the welcome, and especially by the little girl she'd met the day before who held her hand and stayed by her side when the other children were all running around.

They dined on the spit-roasted lamb with okra and tomatoes and smoky eggplant topped with bright red pomegranate seeds and a dozen other salads besides, plus the best bread Amber had ever eaten, all washed down with apple tea and the local white wine.

And afterwards, as the colour drained from the late afternoon sky, everyone took their seats in the big spectator stand and Kadar was introduced to cheers and he climbed onto a podium and gave a speech she couldn't understand a word of, but it was clear the speech was a success, because the crowd was all smiles and cheers and applause and she felt good just being part of the celebration.

Everyone, it seemed, wanted to have a word and shake his hand as he made his way back into the stands and alongside her and he spent time listening to them all. She watched him as he gave them each time, one by one, and felt an insane amount of pride.

Which was mad, because he wasn't hers to be proud of, and she was only here because of his overblown sense of duty, but she was proud all the same. Because she was here, and every now and then it was just nice to forget the real reason why they were together.

He apologised for the delay once he'd managed to reach her side.

'Your workers love you,' she said. 'No boss should ever apologise for that.'

He looked at her strangely, and at the little girl sitting in her lap, and then smiled. 'Wait until you see what's coming next. The best fireworks in the world, made right here in the valley of Burguk.'

As the last of the light leached from the sky they watched a fireworks spectacular the likes of which Amber had never seen. Bright colours lit up the sky in wheels and airbursts and fireballs shooting across the sky, turning night back into day, the air filled with the gasps and cheers of the onlookers, and all overlaid by the ever-present smell of sulphur.

And on her lap sat the little girl—Ayla, she'd learned

her name was—her dark eyes wide with wonder, her mother sitting alongside, a baby wrapped snug in her arms.

When the last of the smoke had drifted away and it was time to hand a now sleepy Ayla back to her family and go, the little girl roused with the motion and put a hand to Amber's hair and said the first words she'd heard her say. She turned to Kadar. 'What did she say?'

'She asked if you're a princess.'

Amber smiled and shook her head at the young girl. 'No. Not a princess. Just an ordinary everyday girl.'

She was anything but ordinary, Kadar thought as they headed back to the Pavilion of the Moon.

Anything but everyday.

And when they went to bed and she handed him the silk scarf to bind her wrists, he said, 'No,' and let the shred of silk flutter to the floor. And she blinked but she turned around and he took her shoulders and turned her back to face him. 'No,' he said again, urging her down upon the big wide bed, before climbing on top. 'No ties this time.'

'But—'

'You haven't recoiled in horror yet. I'm thinking I can handle it if your fingers brush my scars.' He hesitated. 'If you can, that is.'

And she wound her arms around his neck and pulled him into her kiss.

Their lovemaking that night was tender and achingly sweet. He sighed as her fingers stroked the hard nubs of his nipples, growled when her fingernails raked slowly down his sides and reached for him, hard and wanting.

And when he slid into her, Amber almost cried out with the sheer bliss of the connection.

Afterwards, as they lay facing together in the bed,

and Kadar lazily stroked his hand up and back along the curve of her side, he asked her, 'Why did you let a stranger's child sit in your lap?'

She smiled. 'Ayla is sweet. Who could resist her?'

'You have a way with children.'

'Lucky, really, seeing that's what I do.'

'You work with children?'

She dipped her head. 'I teach at a special school in Melbourne, for children who have problems, physically or developmentally. It's good work. Rewarding work.' And a way to help other children when she'd been too unknowing and too young to help Tash.

'That is a noble thing to do,'

'Not noble,' she said, shaking her head, as she told him about her tiny cousin who had died aged barely ten. 'But useful, I hope. I just want to do something that helps.'

'Ah,' he said, 'I see,' and his smile told her he did understand, and his thumb made slow, lazy circles over her hip for a while, so that Amber was almost lured into sleep by his restful touch.

'Ayla has a crooked leg.'

Amber blinked open her eyes and bit her lip. 'I know, I didn't want to ask.'

'I will ask then. Perhaps her family were too shy to ask for help.'

She raised herself up on her elbow. 'Is this your village? Is this where you came from? Is this why you care so much?'

He shook his head. 'My village was further east and much smaller, nominally part of Iran, but so close to the border with Armenia and Azerbaijan that our elders felt beholden to no one.'

She ignored the fact he'd finally answered a question

he'd skirted around that very first day and concentrated on what he hadn't said. 'Was?'

'My village is gone.'

Spider legs of dread crawled down her spine. She thought about the scars on his back. The scars of someone who'd suffered flames, or even worse. 'Fireworks,' she said on a leaden breath.

He didn't say yes or no, just kept sweeping the palm and the fingers of his hands along her side. It should have been soothing—in any other circumstances it would have been soothing—but instead she could feel the weight of the world hovering above his fingertips. The weight of loss. And so she didn't press. She let him take his own time.

'Most of the village was employed in the industry,' he said at length. 'It was illegal, of course, and poorly managed, but it brought a poor village employment and money, hard currency that some insisted be used for health services and schools for the community before improvements in safety. Safety was the responsibility of the owners, some said.

'And it did bring money, for a time, but then it brought death and destruction. Nobody knows what happened—it could have been anything to cause a spark—but they had fireworks stockpiled high for a celebration and something set off a chain reaction. An explosion ripped through the factory, and once started there was no stopping the fire, and no chance for those caught inside, even if they had survived the initial blast.

'My family. My father and mother, my three brothers and my infant sister all perished.'

His hand stopped moving as his words petered out.

'But you, you made it out.'

He took his hand away, looked at her with eyes that

stared at her, both bottomless and empty. 'I had argued with my father that morning. I had pleaded with him that I wanted to go to the new school and learn for a proper job, not go to work in a factory.

'He told me I must work in the factory, alongside my brothers.'

'You shouldn't feel guilty,' she said, 'because you argued. Because you survived. They would not want that.'

'It wasn't that I survived.'

'Then what?'

'It was because I wasn't there.'

'But your burns…'

'I wasn't burnt trying to escape.' He shook his head, his jaw set hard. His eyes weren't empty now. They were filled with pain. Of betrayal. Of loss. Of hurt beyond what was humanly endurable. 'I was trying to get in. To save them.'

She shuddered, her voice a whisper. 'How old were you?'

'Six.'

She swallowed as she attempted to picture it. To imagine. A scene of conflagration, where the world in which you lived had turned into hell, with people trying to escape the fire, to flee, and a small boy running the other way to try to save those he loved.

He turned his gaze towards the constellation of stars built into the ceiling over the bed. 'My mother was upset that morning with the argument I had with my father, the baby crying. I should not argue with my father, she told me, even when I had discussed it with her and she thought one of her children should have a chance at a life in the city. So I pretended to go along with them all and I went to the factory with them, but then, when my father's back was turned, I sneaked away to the school.

I was in my second class when I heard the explosion, when the ground and walls shook and the windows of the new school blew in. And I knew then, that I should be with them.'

Silence surrounded them. A silence hung with sorrow and the horrors of the past.

'Who saved you?' she asked at last.

'I don't know. I didn't get far. I couldn't. All I felt was heat and then something fell on me and then nothing, and the next thing I knew, I woke in a hospital in Istanbul and it hurt so much, I wished I was dead.

'Mehmet found me. He saw the reports in the paper, of a village that had been wiped off the face of the earth, of a child with no family, not expected to live. He called for the best doctors, the best experts. Somehow they brought me back from the brink of death and kept me alive, though there were many times I wished they hadn't bothered. I lost count of the number of operations and skin grafts.'

She shuddered. It would have been excruciating for anyone to bear, let alone a small boy with no family around to support him.

'Mehmet is a good man.'

He rolled onto his stomach, his head on his crossed arms, exposing the tangled scar tissue that was his back in a way that he'd never done before, and it warmed her that he was relaxed enough to do it in front of her now, even while his story chilled. 'The best of men. He schooled me himself until I was strong enough to go. He guided my footsteps. I was lucky.'

Lucky.

It was an odd word for a man who had lost everything and nearly his own life to boot.

She leaned over and tenderly kissed his shoulder at

the place where skin met scar. For a moment he stiffened, and then she felt him relax under her lips.

'Does it still hurt?'

'It pulls.'

And that would hurt. Probably nothing compared to the pain he'd endured through his years of operations, but no doubt more than what most people could bear.

She pressed her lips softly to his skin again, thinking about the damage that could be done when things went wrong and about the people she'd met today, the families and the workers who adored their boss, and shook her head on a sigh.

'What?' he said, rolling back onto his side, lifting her chin with his hand.

'I don't get it,' she said. 'After all that happened to you, how can you even stand the thought of fireworks? And yet you manufacture them. You employ half the valley. What if the same thing happened here?'

'You think I would let that happen to these people? Of course, it can be a dangerous business. But it can also be done safely. There are no children in my factory. No babies. No stockpiles to explode if an accident did happen.'

He curled his hand around her neck, his fingers lacing into her hair, his gaze drinking her slowly in from her toes to her head, making her scalp tingle and setting her senses alight.

But it was the look in his eyes that triggered the flame deep down inside her, once again triggering her need. Dark eyes that burned with their own smouldering heat.

'Don't you see, who better to run a fireworks factory than a man who understands what is at stake if something goes wrong?'

He brushed her hard nipples with the backs of his fingers, turning her skin of her breasts goosebumped as he pulled her head towards his, and she sensed this was madness and could do nothing to stop it.

Who better? she asked herself as he pulled her against his hot mouth.

There was no better.

There was only Kadar.

He lay there under the soft glow from the pinpricks of light from the constellation of stars above the bed, listening to her even breathing, her head on his shoulder, her hair spilled like a river of gold across her pillow, her pale skin pearlescent.

Who was she, this woman who had stumbled into his life and wedged herself in so tight? Who was she, that he would spill the details of his life to her? Details that nobody but his closest friends knew—Zoltan and Bahir and Rashid, his friends from university, and Mehmet, of course, who'd been there and witnessed it all firsthand.

He never thought about children, not having his own, and yet he'd looked at this woman with a child on her lap and he'd seen the woman she would be with her own child—a dark-haired child that he had put in its mother's belly.

Where had that come from?

And why did a few days suddenly seem too short, when he was used to a woman lasting no more than a few hours? Why did the thought of putting her on plane back to her home country make his breath stall and his chest tighten?

He wanted her gone.

He wanted his life back.

He'd wanted those things all along.

And yet...

He looked at her sleeping. A sultan would be proud to have her in his harem. As his favourite.

Why shouldn't he?

No. A sultan wanted progeny. A sultan needed to have a son or preferably a host of sons so that the blood-line could continue.

A sultan needed family.

Kadar didn't.

A family was the last thing he wanted.

Because if you didn't have family, then you couldn't lose them.

He eased her head away and she sighed in her sleep and rolled over, her breathing settling back into regular, while he punched his pillow and cursed the sleep that was proving elusive.

Madness.

Because he wasn't a sultan and he didn't have favourites and he wanted his life back the way it was and nights without a headful of questions.

There was no question about it, no question at all.

It would be better once she was gone.

CHAPTER ELEVEN

AMBER LOVED HER days in the Burguk Valley. When he wasn't needed for meetings with officials or at the factory, Kadar took her sightseeing, showing her the highlights of the wide weather-scoured basin. He took her to other cliffs where in past ages the shepherds had taken shelter and made their homes in the rock as they once had before the Pavilion of the Moon had been carved out the same for a Sultan's retreat. They walked trails along ancient trade routes that took them past centuries-old rock churches, still with frescos of rich reds and golds on the walls and ceilings, and Roman rock tombs and aqueducts.

Today the sky was heavy, the fat dark clouds promising snow that Amber was eagerly anticipating. She'd never seen snow falling, her outer Melbourne suburb too low-lying, and she'd never been in the mountains to witness a snowfall. Strange how she'd had to come all the way to Turkey to see it, but it would be another memory to take home with her.

She was building quite a repertoire of memories to take home with her.

'I never figured you for a tour guide,' she half joked as they walked around the base of the tall pointed rocks he called fairy castles. There were so many sides to

Kadar and this was yet another. Because he'd gone from being someone who seemed to be boss of the town to a man who could relate the history of the valley while they trekked.

'Mehmet used to bring me here,' he explained as they walked. 'Whenever I despaired of life or of how unfair or tough things were, he'd bring me here and we'd walk these paths together. The valley had been here for ever, he'd tell me, and the rocks might be misshapen or bent crooked by the wind but they still stood, tall and proud. It was my choice if I wanted to give in, or to stand resilient like them.'

'Mehmet must be very proud of you.'

'I will never be able to repay him for all that he has done for me.'

She looked at him standing under the dark sky, the cold wind troubling his dark hair, and she understood him better then. She'd imagined he'd always been this way. A leader. Confident and self-assured. But it had been a conscious choice. He could have caved to his loss and his pain and deformity. He could have given in a thousand times to what must have been an agonising journey for a child and a scarred teen trying to find his place in the world, and nobody would have blamed him. But he'd chosen instead to be resilient and to stand tall, to be a leader amongst men.

And she admired him more than ever for it.

Admired?

As the first snowflakes began to fall from the sky, she wished that were all it was. She wished she could summon a hint of the resentment she'd once felt towards him, that she should still harbour towards a man who'd accused her of being a thief. Because instead what she was feeling was a growing respect for the man, and a growing warmth towards him that wasn't all about how good he made her feel in bed.

And it was as inconvenient as it was unwanted, because she hadn't come to Turkey looking for a man, even if she'd somehow managed to stumble upon this very fine example of one. And she certainly hadn't come looking for love.

Which was a damned shame, really.

Seeing that was exactly what she'd found.

God!

She turned into the wind so there was no chance he could read the shock on her features and ask her what was wrong. The icy wind blew a flurry of snowflakes, cold against a face flushed with the heat of her discovery.

She'd been looking forward to the snow. Eagerly anticipating it like a child. Now the thrill of her first snowfall had been overshadowed by the force of something much more momentous. Something altogether more calamitous, the way her heart was racing in her chest.

What the hell was wrong with her? How could she have let it happen? It wasn't supposed to happen!

She felt him take her hand and he whirled her around to face him. 'It's snowing,' he said, with the excitement of someone who knew how much she'd been looking forward to it.

She did her best to smile. 'I know.'

He lifted a hand to her eyes, smoothed a tear from her cheek. 'Then why are you crying?'

She shook her head. 'Because I'm so happy, of course.'

'You look beautiful with snow on your eyelashes,' he said, and kissed her, excited for her, and she tried to feel as excited as him but all she could think was, *No*.

Around them the snow fell heavier, the flakes fatter, turning the landscape white.

'Come,' he said, 'we must go. There's something else you haven't seen yet.'

Back in the warmth of the Pavilion of the Moon, they peeled away their coats and shook off the snow. Kadar took a big set of keys into a locked room set up like those she'd seen in the palaces in Istanbul, with glass display cases to show the treasures of the time and where the students of the nearest university had worked to provide typewritten descriptions in Turkish, Arabic and English. Almost immediately he had to excuse himself to take a phone call, but Amber didn't mind. Because there was so much to see, she wouldn't miss him while she studied the treasures.

There were costumes, exquisite robes of silk and gold, and fine pottery and pouring ware, and there was jewellery of course. Only a fraction of what was on display in the palaces of Topkapi and Dohlmabahce, but the pieces displayed were beautiful nonetheless, the collection the remnants of a sultan's hideaway.

And all of it was magnificent, but it was to the jewellery that her gaze was drawn. There were earrings of pearl and gemstones and armbands of finely worked gold, and bracelets thick and thin, from the simple to the ornate.

And then she saw it.

No!

It shocked her into stillness.

Shocked her into denial so intense she had to close her eyes because she was sure she was imagining it.

Because the bracelet she saw in the cabinet could be hers.

She opened her eyes and it was still there.

Surely it must be hers? Because, if not, it was the closest thing to identical.

But a treasure? She'd always believed it was nothing more than a trinket. Hoped it was nothing more than a trinket. Something her great-great-great-grandmother Amber had picked up in a street market somewhere along her travels.

Oh, God.

Her eyes scanned the description.

A jewelled bracelet of gold and precious gems, ruby, sapphire, emerald and lapis lazuli, from the nineteenth century, one of a pair according to the manufacturer's brief, made as a gift to the Sultan's favourite. The identity of the favourite and the whereabouts of the second bracelet are unknown.

Sensation zipped down her spine, a potent combination of shock and wonder mixed with fear, holding her rooted to the spot. Because she knew the whereabouts of the other bracelet. It was secreted in a pocket of her pack in the room she shared with Kadar.

In the room that the last Amber had shared with the Sultan.

Right here.

She'd actually found her great-great-great-grandmother.

Her ancestor had been here, in this very place, and now, five generations later, she was walking in her shadows and in her footsteps.

The earlier Amber, the favourite of a sultan, no less, and the bracelets a gift from her lover. She'd taken one home and she'd left the other one here—with him?

But why would she have left and gone home to England if she loved him?

There were too many unanswered questions, too many things she still wanted to know. She searched the case, scanning its contents, looking for some other clue but there was none, just the glint of coloured stones—*precious stones*—in the light.

And a chilling thought occurred to her, when she realised her supposedly cheap trinket was none other than a precious Turkish antiquity.

How was she ever going to manage to leave the country with it? It was sure to be found and they would think—

'What have you found?'

She started. She hadn't realised he'd finished his call let alone that he'd caught up with her. *How long had he been watching?* For a split second she toyed with the idea of coming right out and telling him and explaining how she'd found the bracelet in her gran's attic and she'd just found the matching one right here.

But no, she realised, because all along he hadn't trusted her. All along he'd been looking for a reason to prove she was a thief.

He'd assume she'd stolen it, somehow from somewhere. It was better he didn't know. Better he never found out.

'Just some gorgeous pieces of jewellery,' she said with a shrug, moving on along the display.

'Show me.'

'It's nothing,' she said, itching to get out of there as quickly as she could. 'I want to see what's on the other side of this display.' *And then get the hell back to our room and make sure the bracelet is nowhere he can stumble upon it.*

For the first time in days, Kadar sensed trouble. He
didn't really need her to show him. He'd seen her staring at the piece. He'd witnessed her stillness, her intense concentration and the way her hands had balled
as if she was having to stop her fingers reaching out
and taking the piece.

It was no surprise what she was looking at, because
it was like so many pieces that had captured her attention and turned her eyes wide at the palaces in Istanbul
they'd visited. The pieces that combined beaten gold
with coloured gemstones.

And he was disappointed because he'd been beginning to think that he must have been wrong, that he
must have misjudged her after all.

Except here she was, her eyes greedy, her fingers
twitching with excitement.

But why he should feel disappointed, when he'd always taken her for a thief—how did that work?

When had that changed?

Last night, he realised. Right about the time he'd left
her arms unrestrained when he'd made love to her and
she hadn't recoiled when her fingers had touched his tortured back, and he hadn't felt repulsed courtesy of any
horrified reaction. There had been no horrified reaction.

Just a woman holding a man with nothing but passion between them.

It had felt good to hold a woman that way, and to
have her hands hold him. It had felt good to hold Amber
that way.

There was no miracle. He had not forgotten his scars,
because he would never be able to forget them when they
twisted and pulled with every movement, but for once
in his life making love to a woman, he hadn't cared.

He watched her make her way to the other side of the

display case, her fingers trailing along the wooden edge, her blue eyes lingering on an item or to read a description before moving on, making out she was innocence itself, even though he could see the tension around her eyes and in the set of her mouth.

What was going on in her head right now?

She looked up and threw him one of those dazzling smiles that seemed to flick a switch inside him, lighting up all the dark corners inside him, and his body responded the only way it knew.

What was it about her? They had spent days and nights together and still he felt the tug of her body on his. Still he hungered for her as he had that day in the Spice Market.

And for the first time in his life he could remember, he wanted to be wrong.

He didn't want her to be a thief.

Because he didn't want to be able to like someone who was capable of that.

His phone buzzed again and he checked the screen, and excused himself, knowing there was nothing she could do, even if she wanted to.

This place might be no Topkapi, the security systems no way near as sophisticated, but there was no way she was getting her hand on any of the pretties.

Not on his watch.

Three more days, he told himself. Three more nights to enjoy, and then she would be gone.

Then his life could be normal again.

Why didn't that make him feel better?

When he took her to bed that night, she couldn't help but think about the Amber who had gone before. Who had walked these very rooms and slept in this same bed, looking up at the same constellation of stars. She felt her presence everywhere she looked.

Had the Sultan's eyes burned hot as Kadar's did for her?

Had his hands worshipped her, peeling off her clothes, one by one, turning touch into a delicious assault on her senses?

But tonight was no delicious assault and there was no repeat of the tender lovemaking of last night after the fireworks. Instead, there was an edge to their love-making, her fears playing on her mind, the ghost of the Amber of long ago whispering in the darkness, even while Kadar took her body higher and still higher.

And there was a tension in him too. It was there in his tight body and his clenched jaw, and the desperate way he drove into her, again and again, almost as if he were punishing her.

Almost as if he were punishing himself.

But then even the air around them felt tightly sprung and ready to snap, and shimmering with expectation, as if waiting for something to set it off. A room full of mousetraps and ghosts and her mind in the centre of it, spinning in circles around her fears. Kadar. Love. And a bracelet she had to somehow get home.

Love.

And that was the greatest fear of all.

And still Kadar pounded into her, his body sleek with sweat, taking her body inexorably in one direction, the pressure inside her building until her mind had no op-tion but to let go and go with it, and her fears were left spinning aimlessly behind while her mind emptied of everything but sensation and a spiralling need for more.

In the end she didn't come. Not willingly. Her climax was wrenched from her on his cry as he shattered inside her. Not a cry of victory, but an anguished cry that tore at her heart as it sent her hurtling apart.

Tears spilled from her eyes, unwanted, unbidden. Tears that spoke of pointlessness and fear and a love that was never supposed to be.

'Amber?' He cradled her in his arms and his tenderness was so at odds with his lovemaking of before that it only compounded her own anguish. 'Did I hurt you?'

'No,' she said, though she knew he would.

He kissed her forehead, the tip of her nose and her chin before his lips met hers, the briefest, most heart-wrenching brush of lips against lips. 'Then what's wrong?' His breath was warm against her skin, and flavoured with him. She would miss it so when she had gone, and suddenly everything was conspiring to her wretchedness.

'Nothing. Everything.'

He swept the hair from her brow, tendrils that had curled and become glued to her skin in the heated cauldron of their lovemaking. 'What do you mean?'

She sniffed, her mind awhirl, wondering what she could do or say that would make sense of her tears. 'It's nothing. Really, it's nothing.'

'You lost your tour and your money and you didn't cry. You don't strike me as the kind of person to cry over nothing.'

She couldn't tell him of her love or of the bracelet hidden away in her belongings that was a double of one here. Couldn't admit her fears about either. And without a shred of inspiration for what she might make up to account for her tears, instead she licked her lips and said, 'There was a reason I chose Turkey to visit, something I haven't told you. Something that didn't seem important to tell you.'

And she told him of her great-great-great-grand-mother setting off a century and a half before from her home in rural England to journey in a far-off land. Of how she'd disappeared in Constantinople with no trace of her to be found, and how she'd somehow miraculously reappeared five years later, when her family must have assumed her lost for ever, to the feared white slave trade, or worse.

Kadar listened as she explained about the diary she'd found, stained and worn in that attic, where she'd read of the exotic places her gran of so many generations ago wanted to visit. He listened when she explained about the missing pages, torn from the diary, as if her ancestor's story had been so scandalous it had been destroyed.

'What happened to her?'

'Eventually she married a local man and had many children and lived a long life, but, as far as I know, she never travelled again.'

'So why the tears?'

'I came looking for her when I chose Turkey to visit. Wanting to see the sights that she had, wanting to follow in her footsteps. And, I know it will sound strange, but I feel close to her here, in this place.'

'Here?'

'I know,' she said, swiping her cheeks of the tracks of her tears. 'Maybe it's because I'm going home soon, but it's like I've found something of her. A glimpse of where she stepped, or at least what she would have experienced and seen.'

'You should have told me earlier. We could have gone to see some of the places she was excited about seeing.'

She hadn't wanted to tell him. 'I didn't think you'd be interested. Besides, it wasn't like we were friends going on holiday together.' Far from it. She'd been an imposition and she'd been made to feel it. An imposition of convenience, because he'd made no secret of the fact he'd enjoyed their lovemaking.

He pulled her closer into the crook of his shoulder on a sigh. 'Maybe that is true. But still, I don't know why you would cry over it now.'

'I told you it was nothing.'

He kissed the top of her head. 'I thought I had hurt you.'

'No,' she assured him as the tiny lights in the constellation above the bed winked down at her knowingly.

That would come later.

CHAPTER TWELVE

THE FLIGHT BACK to Istanbul was unremarkable, the turbulence of the thin winter air as they rose over the mountains no match for the turbulence going on inside him.

The days they'd spent at Burguk had been some of his best. He should know. His best days were easy to find.

Days spent in the company of his desert brothers. At the university where the foursome, initially resentful at being thrust together, had forged a bond made of steel. At their occasional adventures since then—with Bahir introducing them to the excitement of the casinos and the games of chance at which he somehow excelled, and with Zoltan racing across the desert sands to save the princess Aisha from the clutches of the warped and power-crazed Mustafa.

Days when the four were together to celebrate first Zoltan's and then Bahir's weddings.

Good days.

And now the few nights spent at the Pavilion of the Moon with a woman whose smile could outshine the sun and stars.

Could outshine the sun and stars.

But the last few days… He looked across at her in

the business-class seat alongside him. Her eyes were closed and yet still he could see the tension that had been hovering in the background like a dark threatening cloud.

What was it that was troubling her?

What was it lingering behind her smile, dimming the lights he'd become accustomed to seeing?

Because she would still smile when she caught him looking but other times she was nervous. Ever since that night she'd burst into tears.

Because of the story of her ancestor?

Why hadn't she mentioned it before? They hadn't been close at the start, but these last few days a bond had grown between them.

And why had she felt her here, more than, say, in Istanbul, where her ancestor was far more likely to have stepped?

Something wasn't right, and it was troubling her, and that troubled him.

He sighed and leaned back in his chair as the 'fasten seat belt' light lit up again and the plane hit another patch of turbulence. It was just as well she was going. She'd been a pleasant distraction—too pleasant at times, but a distraction all the same. It would be good to concentrate on his business and his life again without having to cater to a guest's demands.

Not that she'd demanded much. On the contrary, he'd foisted himself upon her and she'd been the one who'd had to endure his terms and conditions.

He would miss her when she was gone.

So it was just as well she was leaving.

Amber curled her legs under her in her wide seat and closed her eyes, the bumpy air only reinforcing the bumpy thoughts in her mind. She'd come here searching for a glimpse of the adventure her great-great-great-grandmother had discovered, but she'd never imagined when she'd left home that her trip here would find hard evidence of her.

Amber Braithwaite. She'd been at the Pavilion of the Moon and worn bracelets fashioned for the Sultan's favourite. A favourite of the Sultan. How hard it must have been to settle back into life in rural Hertfordshire after such an adventure. How hard it must have been for her family to understand.

She thought about the missing pages of the diary, which looked as if they'd been torn out. Was that why someone had disposed of them? So that news of the scandalous adventures of their daughter could never be made public?

Follow your heart.

Amber settled deeper into the leather seat, those three little words playing over in her mind. She would never answer all the questions, she would never know how the Amber of long ago had come to be at the Pavilion of the Moon, but she would never regret coming to Turkey, never. No matter what happened next. Because she'd found her intrepid ancestor. Found where she'd been while she'd been lost those five long years, and where she'd loved a man who could never be hers.

Never had she felt so close to her namesake—so close they could have been sisters rather than being born generations apart.

For she too had followed her heart, and lost it.

She squeezed her eyes shut as turbulence jolted the plane and the wings bent against the bumpy clouds.

'It's okay,' said Kadar, putting a hand to her arm.

And she wished it could be true.

* * *

She was leaving, right this minute packing her bags, ready for the drive to the airport and her flight home. Kadar stood at the rain-streaked windows of his apartment and looked out over the Sea of Marmara, grey under a heavy sky, the ships mere smudges of colour that failed to break up the monotony of sea and sky.

He should feel relieved.

He wanted to be relieved.

Instead he felt—*uneasy*.

In the days and nights they'd been together, he'd grown used to having her around.

More than that, he'd grown to like having her around.

And more and more that particular thought had found a foothold in his head.

He would miss her.

Her eyes. Her smile. The way she came apart in his arms like fireworks. And in spite of his initial mistrust of her and his doubts about her character, there were things about her that he did like. The way she wooed the hearts of the villagers. The way he'd found her peeling oranges surrounded by a mob of children.

And beyond staring at pretty jewellery behind glass, she'd done nothing that he could find her guilty of.

After all, even he had to admit, it was no crime to look.

Had she been as innocent and naive of knowing she'd been committing a crime with the coin seller as she'd made out?

Had he unfairly cast a stain upon her character all along? If she was as opportunist as he had believed, surely she would have been unable to resist the lure of some other trinkets? The Pavilion of the Moon was full of treasures, large and small. If she'd wanted some souvenirs of her time in Turkey, she'd had plenty of opportunity.

He chewed it over in his mind, trying to make sense of this woman who'd come into his life unwanted and unwilling, and was now consuming his thoughts.

Why?

Did it really matter if he'd been wrong about her? If he'd misjudged her?

No, it didn't matter. She was going home. They'd never see each other again. If she hadn't stolen anything, it didn't matter the reason why. And if something was troubling her, that was her problem, not his. He'd still done the job he'd promised the *polis*. He'd been responsible for her. He'd ensured she would cause no more trouble while she was in the country.

He'd discharged his duty.

So maybe he'd given her grief over it, but she'd asked for that, messing with the coin seller in the first place. That was hardly his fault. What other conclusion could anyone have drawn?

He ran his hand through his hair and turned away from the window, unsatisfied with his cold justification for his behaviour. Because if she had been innocent all along then he had treated her appallingly, unafraid to accuse her in front of anyone in hearing distance that she was a thief.

Even if only at first.

He thought back to that morning with Mehmet and how angry she'd been. Deservedly angry.

He'd appointed himself judge, jury and executioner and, sure, he'd been trying to dissuade Mehmet from the notion that she actually meant something to him, but even that rationalisation seemed hollow now.

Because she wasn't nothing to him. He'd miss her

when she was gone. You didn't miss people who meant nothing to you. You were happy to see them walk out of your life and go.

But not Amber. And the closer it got to her leaving, the more uneasy, the more unsettled, he became.

It was because of those good days, he reflected. A string of the best days of his life, that would be followed by a life without Amber.

It was akin to contemplating life without the sun. Unimaginable.

And yet that was what he was setting himself up for by letting her calmly walk out of his life—a life full of empty days, of going back to women that were repulsed when they saw his scars and eagerly turned their backs on him, of going back to women who seemed grateful they didn't have to touch his skin. A life full of brief, meaningless encounters.

Amber had kissed him there. On his shoulder, where skin met scar. Amber had traced the ridges of his scars with her fingertips. Not in pity, or in morbid curiosity, but because that was the way he was and she accepted him the way he was.

Oh, God, he was such a fool.

He wasn't just going to miss her.

He didn't want her to go.

He strode the wide living room, the sky and sea merging into one in the windows outside, his thoughts in turmoil.

What was this feeling? What was wrong with him?

Because suddenly he wanted his days to be filled with her.

He wanted to spend his life with her.

His chest ached, his gut churned, his brow broke out in a cold sweat as the sick knowledge dawned on

152 CAPTIVE OF KADAR

him, a sick knowledge he denied as fast as the realisation dawned.

Because he wasn't supposed to fall in love.

He wasn't supposed to love anyone.

And yet, Amber had arrived and all the rules he'd lived by had meant nothing.

Because he loved her.

He raised his eyes up to the ceiling. Oh, God, he had to stop her going. He couldn't just let her walk out of his life. He had to do something.

But what if she wouldn't stay? What if this was all one-sided? She was on the rebound. She wasn't looking for love, she'd said.

And then he thought about the last few days, when something had clearly been troubling her, something that she hadn't been able to share with him, that had dimmed the light in her eyes and had taken the edge off her smile.

She'd cried that night after they'd made love. She'd told him the story of her ancestor then to explain away her tears and it had never really made sense to him why she was so moved.

But if she'd told him the story because she'd needed to tell him *something* to explain away her tears?

Because she couldn't tell him the real reason?

Because she was no more looking forward to leaving than he was to her going home...

Was there a chance?

Did she feel something for him?

Could she have fallen in love with him? Might that explain the tension around her troubled eyes?

He didn't know much about love, but it made a kind of sense that she would be as averse to divulging her feelings as he was. No doubt more so, given the way he'd ridden roughshod over her wants and insisted on calling the shots from day one.

She had reason to resent him right there. And yet their lovemaking had been nothing but explosive. Could love be born into such a mixture? Was it even possible?

He looked towards the bedroom where she was packing the last of her things as his phone beeped. His driver, letting him know he and the car were only five minutes away.

He had to talk to her.

Would she listen?

Would she want to hear what he had to say?

But in the end, he thought as he strode towards the bedroom, it didn't matter.

Because he had to try.

Her time in Turkey was at an end. Amber packed the last of her things, preparing for her flight home later that evening. It was the bracelet that brought her out in a sweat. Where to pack it? Stashed away in her luggage and risk it being stolen if it wasn't picked up on X-ray, or in her hand luggage and almost guarantee it would be detected.

Flying out with it was so much more of a risk than flying in. An X-ray machine was bound to find it. Why hadn't she just left it at home?

But then, she'd never had any idea.

That had been her problem all along. Having no idea had got her into trouble with the coin seller. Having no idea had seen her bring a bracelet that she should have left at home.

She sat on the bed, turning the bracelet in her hands. The other Amber's bracelet. The adventurous one's.

Strange to think that, when her own visit had turned out to be nothing but an adventure.

She slipped the bracelet on her wrist and the jewels glinted in the light, and she smiled, thinking of her courageous ancestor, looking at these same stones, the gift from a sultan…

'Amber, before you go…'

Kadar's voice shattered her thoughts, his presence turning them to disarray. Instinctively she swiped her arm behind her back. 'Almost done.'

He stopped dead. His eyes narrowed. Troubled eyes that now swirled with suspicion. Her stomach flipped.

'Is everything all right?'

'Sure. Just a few last bits and pieces to go. I'll, er, be with you in a second.'

His eyes honed in on the arm still held behind her back. She swivelled a little on the bed so she didn't look as unnatural as she felt, her heart tripping over itself as if in a bid to get away. She wanted to run with it.

His head tilted, his focus one hundred per cent on the arm that she dared not move, and she cursed herself for the impulse that had made her slip it on. 'What have you got there?'

'Nothing.'

'No,' he said, coming closer. 'There was something. So I'll give you another chance to tell me. What have you got behind your back?'

His voice was low and purposeful and threatening and made her thoughts all but curdle. If she'd been frightened before about how to hide her bracelet for the journey home, it was nothing to how she felt now. It would be a miracle if she even made it to the airport with it.

And then another thought chilled her to the bone.

It would be a miracle if she made it to the airport, period.

And because she knew the best form of defence was attack and because she had nothing to lose, and because he was so damned tall, she raised her chin defiantly as she stood and turned away from him, hiding her wrist before her now, and said, 'It is nothing that concerns you. Nothing you need concern yourself with.'

He followed her as she moved on shaky knees towards the window. 'Show me!'

'No!'

'Why not?'

'Because you will think the worst of me if I do! Because you will jump to conclusions like you always do!'

He made a sound like a growl, low and threatening behind her, making her knees quiver and her lip tremble. 'Do I have to pull you around and see for myself?'

She blinked furiously as tears pricked at her eyes, searching for escape. But before her was a window and behind her was Kadar and there was nowhere to flee. 'Why can't you just trust me, for once?'

'How can I, when you hide something from me that you know will make me angry? And why will it make me angry, I wonder? Unless it supports everything I ever thought about you.'

She looked over her shoulder at him, his face so angry, so contorted with rage, and she didn't want him to be angry. She didn't want him to rage. But she knew he would. She knew there could be nothing but rage now.

And it scared the hell out of her that there was not a thing she could do to prevent it.

He took a step closer and she gasped at the set of his shoulders and the determination in his features. He looked as if he would tear her limb from limb.

'Okay, I'll show you,' she said in a rush as she cringed closer to the window. 'But before I do, you have to know that this is mine,' she said, keeping her hand clutched tight over her wrist. 'You need to know that. It's mine.'

His eyes didn't so much as flicker, his jaw set rock hard as slowly she turned and lifted her hand from her wrist. 'I brought it here. It's *mine*.'

Her fingers lifted and he saw the glint of colour and gold and the bottom dropped out of his newly constructed world. Because it was the bracelet. The one she'd been unable to drag her eyes from in the display at the Pavilion of the Moon. And every cell in his body turned around and pointed at him and said *fool*!

'How did you pull this off? How did you manage to steal it?' he demanded, almost unable to rasp the words out, he was so overcome by his own stupidity. He'd been going to come in here and tell her that he couldn't bear to live without her. That she should stay. That he loved her. And now—this?

And grief for the loss of the dream he'd been building in his mind, and anger that he had been so stupid to ever imagine he could love her when he had known all along that she was a thief, all of it combined into one huge tidal wave of fury that rolled over him and turned his vision red.

'I didn't steal it!'

He thrust out his hand. 'Give it to me.'

'No! I told you, the bracelet is mine!'

She shook her head and pulled her wrist against her chest with her other hand. She was trembling now, her blue eyes wide and filled with fear, as well they might, because she should feel afraid right now.

'It's the bracelet you were staring at in the case at the

Pavilion of the Moon. You saw it and you lusted after it and you stole it.'

'No! It looks the same, I know. But it was Amber's. My great-great-great-grandmother's. I told you about her, remember? She disappeared for five years and when I saw the bracelet in the display I was struck with it—of course I was. Because I'd found her. I found where my ancestor had been.'

And he laughed, if you could call the grating sound he made a laugh. 'Oh, yes, of course, I remember. You told me about her, *after* you'd seen the bracelet and decided to steal it, that is. It was a fabrication, so you'd have an excuse all ready in case you were caught.'

'No! It's the truth. It was her bracelet. I found it with her diary when I was helping clean out my grandmother's attic.'

'Show me this diary, then, if what you are telling me is true.'

'I don't have it. I didn't bring it.'

'And yet you brought the bracelet?'

'The diary is too fragile! It never would have survived the trip.'

'How convenient.'

'It's the truth! Have them check at the Pavilion of the Moon. Call someone. Get them to check. The bracelet is still there, I swear. The label says there were originally two, made for the Sultan's favourite. Amber must have been that favourite. She took one home to England with her. She must have left one behind here for whatever reason.'

'Of course, she did.' He flicked his fingers. 'I'm still waiting.'

'Didn't you read what it said? Didn't you see the caption?'

He shook his head, as amazed by her sheer brazen-ness as he was by his own stupidity. He'd almost be-lieved there might be a kernel of truth in what she'd said. Because he'd wanted to believe what she said was true. Fool! 'How long did it take to come up with this pack of lies? Did you make it up on the spot or did you fabricate it all before you came, so you would be ready to wheel out your so sad and mysterious tale of your ancestor in case you got caught? Were the tears part of your plan, so that I would be so touched by your depth of emotion, I would have to be swayed to believe you?'

'It's the truth!'

'You lie! For the last time, give me the bracelet!'

Her beautiful face crumpled. Beautiful thieving face, he thought, correcting himself as she twisted off the bracelet over her hand and finally passed it to him. The metal was warm where it had rested against her skin, and he wished it as cold as he felt towards her right now. 'Please listen, Kadar, you've just got to believe me.'

'Believe the words of a common thief? Anyone would have to be a fool to believe you.' He snorted. 'And I al-most did. I almost thought I'd been wrong about you, sweet little Amber Jones. I almost thought you were something special, you know that? God, I'm a fool.'

She blinked up at him, her eyes filled with tears.

'No! I can't believe you were so stupid. I told you it was illegal to deal with Turkish antiquities. And still you couldn't help yourself. Get your things together. My driver will take you to the airport. And the only reason I don't have you delivered to the nearest *polis* station is because I'm sick to death of the sight and sound of you. Always feigning innocence when you've been nothing more than a common thief the whole time. The sooner you're gone, the better.'

'Take me to the *polis*, then. Take me there and I will explain—'

'And who do you think they are going to believe? You, who has already come to their attention for trying to deal in antiquities, or me? You will be thrown in jail before you know it. Be grateful that I am letting you go.'

She sniffed. 'Fine,' she said, snatching up her bag and pulling out a notepad and a pen. 'Be a bastard. That's what you're best at, after all.' She scrawled her name and address on a piece of paper and thrust it at him. 'When I am gone, and you discover the mistake you have made, this is where you can return my brace-let to me.'

He swiped it from her proffered hand and balled it in his fist, flinging it onto the floor.

'I think we both know I won't be needing that.'

CHAPTER THIRTEEN

KADAR STEWED IN his empty apartment for two entire days being constantly reminded of where Amber wasn't to be found. Wearing an achingly short checked cloth in his shower. In the bed he'd grown used to seeing her in. Against the glass doors while she counted the ships sailing by as he…

She wasn't in any of those places, but he saw her all the same.

So he would put his coat on and shove his hands deep down in his pockets and he would walk the windy, rain-streaked streets of Istanbul, walk till he was sure her ghost must finally be gone, only to go home and find himself still sensing her in the movement of a shadow, still catching her perfume when he least expected it.

Two days of torture and he was over it. He'd done the right thing, hadn't he? He'd cut off the offending limb and cauterised the wound. So why was this black mood hanging over him like a dark cloud?

Because he was still angry at himself, he reasoned. Because she'd lied to him and he'd almost fallen for it. Almost imagined that she was special, and that he would be a fool to let her go.

Lying sleepless and alone at three in the morning in his big wide bed, he knew the truth.

He was a fool, and it wasn't because he'd let her go.

Because with Amber, he'd actually believed the impossible—that it was possible for him to feel love for a woman. Love with Amber, at any rate.

Fool!

He'd let a liar and a thief work her clever cunning way into his heart, and if anything he should feel relieved.

Maybe what he needed was a change of scenery.

He thought about visiting his three friends, even just for a couple of days for a change of scenery, but Zoltan and Bahir were married and had young families and he would be a third wheel, and besides, his friends weren't stupid. One of them was bound to sniff out that there was something on his mind. Something he'd rather not confess.

And God only knew where Rashid was in the world at the moment. Which was a shame, because he could do with talking to another confirmed bachelor right now. The competitiveness between them alone would have been enough to convince him he was better off without her.

Fed up with his mind going in ever-decreasing circles, he left his meeting with the advertising agency that wanted to use his fireworks, and had his driver pull up outside the Spice Market. He would visit Mehmet and tell him of his time in Burguk and his visit to the Pavilion of the Moon.

Maybe a visit to his old friend would brighten his dark mood.

But the Spice Market only reminded him of Amber and those red jeans and blue eyes and a smile that could light up the marketplace, and he scowled at the man serving him the dates and apple tea as if it were all his fault, and left the market in an even darker mood.

Mehmet at least was happy to have a visitor. It was something. 'I brought you apple tea and some dates. Would you like some tea now or would you prefer coffee?'

Mehmet waved his thanks. 'Come in, come in. It is good to see you, my friend.' He cocked an ear. 'But you are alone?'

'Of course, I am alone.'

'And your friend?'

He ground his teeth together. 'Amber left two days ago.'

'Oh, I am sorry to hear that. I liked your young woman.'

'She was never my young woman,' he growled, already heading for the kitchen, making an executive decision. 'I'll make us some tea.' Sure, maybe for one moment he'd almost fallen for her wiles. For one second he'd imagined—but no. He was never cut out for love and marriage and family. He'd been a fool to forget that for even a second.

Besides, she was a thief. An opportunist. He'd known it from the start and she'd proved him right. When all was said and done, he'd had a lucky escape. Mehmet himself had had a lucky escape. Which reminded him, as he boiled water and made tea for them in copper pots, and found a dish for the dates, he still had to get the bracelet back to the Pavilion of the Moon. Strange that nobody had missed it, but then, the university students cataloguing the collection might still be on holidays. Maybe that was where he should go. Not that visiting the Pavilion of the Moon would make him forget about Amber. Her ghost would be everywhere there.

He poured the tea into glass cups and took it and the dates through to the other room.

'The dates are just how you like them, old friend,' he said, finding a space on a side table in the old man's reach. 'Plump and meaty.'

Mehmet took one and nibbled on it with his old teeth and nodded. 'Excellent. You are good to an old man.'

And Kadar knew he was only giving him back a fraction of what he'd done for him and so much less than what he deserved if he were ever to repay him, but he smiled anyway. He was right to come. The visit was working. He felt better already.

'As I said,' the old man said, 'I'm sorry your friend has had to go home.'

'Yes,' Kadar said resignedly, knowing he would feel better when the old man had finished with that particular subject. Mehmet was bound to be disappointed when he had all but decided that Amber was going to become some kind of permanent fixture in Kadar's life on the basis of a ten-minute meeting with her. Any meeting would have been built into something else by Mehmet. But he'd save him the truth. He wouldn't tell him how close he'd come to being right. But neither would he share that she was indeed a thief and that he'd caught her stealing from even him. He didn't need to hear the whole truth. 'You did say that.'

'Will you see her again, do you think?'

'No.' Not if he had anything to do with it. She lived in a country on the other side of the globe and, after her deception and the betrayal of his trust, even that did not seem far enough away. 'There is no chance of that.'

'Oh. For that I am sorry. I was hoping to show her something I found. How will she see it now?'

Kadar was only half interested. He flicked his hand at a piece of lint on his trousers. 'What did you find?'

'Because I remembered after your visit why she seemed so familiar.'

Kadar stiffened, the whole of his attention with the old man's words now, and he had the distinct feeling his dark mood wasn't going to be getting any better any time soon. Even though the old man's sight was negligible, there were things he perceived that went beyond sight. 'Familiar? You never mentioned that before.'

He shrugged. 'I could not be sure. Not at first. My mind is not what it used to be. It was the name that struck me. An unusual name. And then I remembered.'

He turned to the side and fussed with some bits and pieces he had sitting there while Kadar waited, uncertainty setting needles under him in the upholstery of his chair so that everywhere his body made contact with it prickled.

His tea sat untouched in the wait.

'Ah.' Mehmet picked something up, something flat but too small for Kadar to make out, and ran his fingertips over the surface, and his face lit up as he nodded. 'Yes. I am certain.' He passed what was in his hand to Kadar. 'What do you think?'

Kadar took it with a growing sense of foreboding, his blood starting to thicken and curdle in his veins. But it was only when his heart lurched when he glanced down at the small oval disc in his hand that he realised it was justified.

It was her.

His mind told him it couldn't be.

And yet it was. Amber's profile, carved from layers of shell, white against the caramel-coloured surround.

And the worst of it was, it didn't look recent. It looked old. Antique.

'Where did you get this?'

'From my father.'

And a shiver ran through Kadar from his scalp to his toes.

'But it's her. It's Amber.'

'I knew it!' Mehmet declared, slapping his hand against his thigh, suddenly brighter, 'I thought the same. That is why I asked you if she'd been to Istanbul before. Because I was sure I'd encountered her features somewhere before. It was right here, in this cameo.'

And the gears and cogs of Kadar's mind groaned and shifted as a sickening feeling settled thickly upon an already black mood. He didn't want to entertain such a thing could be possible because then he'd have to consider that the stories Amber had spun might have contained a kernel of truth.

He did not want to have to admit that.

Because then he'd be forced to admit that maybe he'd been wrong about the bracelet too.

He could not have been wrong about the bracelet.

She was a thief. He was certain of it.

He was counting on it.

That was the reason he hadn't returned the bracelet yet. Because in a small dark corner of his mind, he'd known that he couldn't risk it, that he'd feared what she'd said might be true and that he might find the bracelet he'd accused her of stealing still there in the cabinet under lock and key. He'd clung to the belief that she had stolen it because the alternative was too horrible to contemplate.

But if she wasn't a thief…

'Did your father tell you who this was?'

'There is a story he told me. Not written in the official histories of the court or the harem, so no trace of her will be found there, that there was a woman who came from the West, with blond hair and blue eyes and who was found wandering lost and alone, and sick with fever, after her tour party was raided, the horses and camels stolen, her guides lost or murdered.' He shrugged. 'Nobody knew.

'She was taken to the Pavilion of the Moon, where the Sultan happened to be visiting.

'The harem was back at the palace, no women accompanied him for this was a place of reflection and prayer. But he took the woman in and she recovered and became his secret desert wife. His business was at the palace, his visits to her necessarily infrequent given the distance, but in time she bore him a child. A daughter. Fortuitous for her, because by now her existence was whispered of in the palace, and if she'd borne him a son she and the child would most certainly have been killed. As it was, her presence was tolerated only because she had no impact on the succession. Alas, the child ailed and died in infancy.

'A year later, and it was the Sultan himself, who died. He had left instructions before his death that the woman be sent home, because it would be too dangerous for her to remain.

'My father arranged as the Sultan had commanded. She pressed this brooch into his hand as she made her thanks to him and boarded the ship that would take her home.'

Kadar's gut was churning, his thoughts in turmoil, as he asked the question he did not want to hear the answer to. 'What was the name of this woman, do you know?'

'They called her Kehribar.'

A muscle in Kadar's jaw popped.

The Turkish word for amber.

A coincidence. Surely it was a terrible coincidence.

'Did she take anything with her when she left?'

Mehmet thought for a moment and then nodded. 'Ah, yes. Whatever made you think of that? I had forgotten that part of the story. There were two bracelets the Sultan had fashioned for her as a gift. Kehribar asked my father that he place one bracelet in the Sultan's tomb, as an eternal memory of her, while the other she would keep close to her heart. Alas, that would not be tolerated, so the bracelet was returned to the Pavilion of the Moon, where it remains today.'

As it surely did.

Two bracelets, then. And the woman had taken one and her descendant had unwittingly brought it back, only to be accused of stealing it.

Only for Kadar to accuse her of stealing it.

She'd been telling him the truth all along.

Oh, God, what had he done?

'She told me a story,' he said, the words of his admission having to all but chisel their way out through his rock-hard throat, 'that an ancestor of hers had travelled to Constantinople where she'd disappeared only to turn up on the family doorstep more than five years later. When I found her with a bracelet of gold and jewels, I told her she was lying. That she'd made up a story to cover her tracks. That the bracelet she had said she had brought with her was stolen. From the Pavilion of the Moon.'

'And did you check to see if that particular bracelet was still there?'

'No.' Because they'd been back in Istanbul by then and he hadn't needed to anyway, or so he'd thought. Because he'd been convinced it was the same one. He'd seen her gazing longingly at it in the display case, her eyes wide, her lips parted, and that had been his proof. He'd interpreted her shock—her discovery—as lust, pure and simple.

And he hadn't been in any hurry to check if the bracelet was still there, because he hadn't wanted to discover that she'd been telling the truth the whole time.

'I was wrong,' he said. But, God, how wrong? He remembered her defiance when he'd found her with the bracelet. Her defiance. Her tears. He remembered his unwavering certainty. She'd begged him to listen, and he hadn't. She'd pleaded with him to check the bracelet was still there and he hadn't. He remembered her scribbling down her address so he could return the bracelet when he discovered she'd been telling the truth and he'd screwed it up and flung it away as easily as he'd discarded the feeling in his heart that she was special. He hadn't given her a chance. 'I've never been so wrong. But it's worse than that, Mehmet. Because I wronged her.'

The old man made a rasping scratchy sound, half sigh, half recrimination, or that was the way that Kadar read it, because it was a sound that grated on what was left of Kadar's conscience. 'And what comes next, my young friend?'

There was no question in Kadar's mind.

'There is something I must do.' He looked at the antique brooch in his hand. 'Can I take the cameo?'

Mehmet nodded. 'You must. After all, it is rightfully hers.'

CHAPTER FOURTEEN

AMBER WAS GOING to have to find herself a new flat, and soon. She sat wrapped in her summer silk dressing gown, fresh from her shower, in the dining room of the suburban home her parents had owned for more than thirty years. It was generous of them to welcome her back into the family home, seeing she'd gladly left Cameron and the flat they'd shared for a year before her shock discovery, but a permanent proposition, it was not.

Especially when news of her return got around the neighbourhood. Because if one more friendly neighbour happened to drop by while her mum and dad were at work with a batch of scones or a casserole to console her about the boyfriend and best friend who weren't, she'd go mad.

'Are you over it all, dear?' they'd ask, with cups poised over saucers and ears poised for all the gory details. 'Did Turkey get it all out of your system or are you still feeling upset over the whole sorry affair?'

And who could blame them, because of course she looked like she was still upset? She had bags under her eyes from not sleeping and jet lag was only to blame for a fraction of that.

But how could she tell them Cameron hadn't figured

in her thoughts since she'd met a dark-eyed god who'd rocked her world, even if only for a while? Until, that was, she'd been spat out like a pit from a date.

How could she explain that her grief was caused by something else entirely? Something else a whole lot worse.

Because in a few short days and nights, and against her own better judgement, she'd fallen in love with Kadar.

Crazier still, he'd even imagined that he'd felt something for her.

Only to have been rejected, coldly and absolutely, and ejected from his life and his country like a common criminal.

She should hate him for that. She should hate him for not believing her and for taking her precious bracelet from her. Precious because of its history and what it had meant to her great-great-great-grandmother.

And she did hate him. She hadn't stopped hating him since she'd been practically frogmarched onto her plane home and summarily dismissed from his life.

But somehow it wasn't the anger or hatred that stayed uppermost in her mind where she wanted it. It was grief for something lost.

For something fragile that had been found in the heat of their torrid nights.

Something that had been both scary and precious.

At least that was how it had felt to her.

She skimmed through the Accommodation Vacant column and drew a circle around a likely looking flat just as the doorbell rang.

She rolled her eyes and put her pen down. Her parents were both at work and her brother had headed down to the beach with his mates, and if this was another kindly neighbour coming to see how she was, she'd go mad. The sooner she could find her own flat, the better.

She lashed her robe more tightly around her as she headed for the door. At least she had an excuse to say this was a bad time and not to invite whoever it was in for coffee.

She opened the door no more than a scant few inches and peeked around the edge, only to have her world judder to a halt.

No way!

She blinked, thinking she must have imagined him, conjured the vision up from her recent thoughts, but when she opened her eyes he was still there, and her world was still reeling from its sudden stop, her stomach flip-flopping with it, desperately seeking a new balance. And the dark eyes watching her looked so troubled and anguished that all she could think was that he had come for her...

'How did you find me?' Her heart was hammering in her chest. He'd thrown her address away when she'd tried to give it to him.

'I was at the *polis* station, remember, when you were interviewed.'

'And you remembered?'

His dark eyes gave nothing away, but for the first time she noticed the lines around them. Jet lag? Or something else?

'Can I come in?'

She kept the door precisely where it was and clutched her wrap more tightly at the neck, wishing she'd finished getting dressed before being distracted by flat hunting. Wishing she'd dried her hair. Wishing she could have flung the door open looking confident and happy rather than like this cowering half-baked mess of woman. And that thought alone was enough to give her some backbone. Because this was her patch. She had nothing to cower from here. 'Why? What do you want?' And almost immediately it struck her that her momentary flight of fancy was nothing but a case of wishful thinking, and there could be no other reason he could be back. 'Did you bring me back my bracelet?'

A muscle in his jaw popped. 'Yes.'

Realistically, it was the most she could have wished for and more than she'd expected as the days had gone by. Still, somehow, it didn't seem anywhere near enough. 'So what took you so long?' She didn't care that she sounded grumpy. He would have realised he'd made a huge error the first moment he'd checked with the staff at the Pavilion of the Moon.

'Can we talk about this inside?'

She looked at him standing on her doorstep, tall and imposing and more starkly handsome even than she dreamed about at night in her narrow single bed. Gone were the cashmere coat and the long-sleeved silky knits that hugged his form. He was dressed for summer here, in a short-sleeved polo that skimmed his chest and flat abs, and cool chinos. With dark hair pushed back and with just a shadow of stubble on his chin, he looked cool and urbane, the flash black car with driver waiting for him in the driveway a dead giveaway that this man did not belong in this world. She could imagine curtains up and down the street twitching, and figured letting him inside was the lesser of two evils. After all, he was bringing her back her bracelet.

She pulled the door open and let him pass, felt her skin prickle with his nearness, and almost instantly regretted letting him inside. The door between them had felt solid and real whereas now there was just the quivering air and nothing to hold on to but her own trembling arms.

For the little lounge room, perfectly adequate in size to hold her parents and her brother, suddenly seemed too small, the ceiling too low, the space shrunken around him.

She watched him uneasily from behind as he surveyed the contents of the room, his gaze taking in the photographs and tiny crystal animals her mum collected lined up on the mantelpiece over the gas heater. Photos of her and her brother in their school uniforms from way back when. A photo of the family on the beach together one Christmas holiday long ago and her parents' wedding picture. Plus a photo of Amber at her graduation a couple of years back wearing her robe and black mortar board, proudly displaying her new degree, her wrist proudly wearing her ancestor's bracelet. Between them all was scattered a veritable zoo of crystal animals that sparkled as they caught the light.

All of it so normal to her. So humble. And it occurred to her that their worlds were so far apart, he must be wondering what he'd struck.

She swallowed as he picked up the photo of her smiling so brightly in her graduation robe, the bracelet that had been the subject of so much emotion and misunderstanding, and the silence in the room stretched to breaking point.

'So—my bracelet?'

He stilled and put the photo down, running his hand through his hair as he turned, his eyes looking almost tortured as he retrieved a satin pouch from his pocket and withdrew her bracelet. He'd had it polished, she realised as she took it, the gold and the stones gleaming as if it were new.

Hello, old friend, she thought as her fingers curled around it, because she'd imagined it lost for all time. 'So you checked with the Pavilion of the Moon, then?'

Why was she so calm? Why didn't she yell at him, scream at him, demand the apology she so richly deserved? The bracelet clearly meant the world to her. He'd known that even before he'd seen her graduation picture. So why didn't she rail against his injustice?

As it was, it was all he could do not to drag her into his arms where he wanted her to be. With her tousled hair and in a silken knee-length robe that slipped apart at the neck to reveal a hint of lace beneath, she looked as if she was ready to tumble into bed, and how he longed to. But there were smudges too, under her eyes, he'd put those smudges there, and he had no right to tumble her anywhere after what he had done. No right at all.

'I did check,' he said, 'but not before I already knew the truth.'

'How?' She clutched the bracelet to her chest, as she had that day in Istanbul when he'd caught her with it and she'd told him it was hers and pleaded with him to believe her, and that picture of him and the knowledge that he'd done that to her wrenched his gut Now he could see what it meant to her and what it must have cost her when he'd ripped it away, and he felt even more of a bastard than he had before.

And he wished he could have said that he'd never really believed she could have stolen it—that the moment she'd gone he'd realised what a fool he'd been. But that wasn't how it had happened at all, and he hated himself for it.

'Mehmet,' he said. 'Who told me a story of a young

woman who had been found lost and alone and who had become the Sultan's favourite right there in the Pavilion of the Moon.'

'I knew it,' she whispered, clutching the bracelet tighter. 'I knew it. I felt her there.'

'She'd been abandoned,' he told her, 'with no sign of her tour guides or her party. But the Sultan took her in to ensure she was cared for, and in the end they became lovers.

'And this,' Kadar said, handing her the cameo, 'is what proves it beyond doubt.'

She took it warily, questions swirling in her blue eyes, blue eyes that suddenly widened. 'Oh, my God!'

She had to sit down before she fell down. 'It could be me.'

'I know.' Kadar related the story as Mehmet had told him, of her life with the Sultan, of the reason she had been sent home to England, and of the tiny child, the daughter who hadn't survived. He told her how the earlier Amber had asked for one of the bracelets to remain and how she'd gifted Mehmet's father the cameo in thanks.

He told her that she had been known as Kehribar, the Turkish word for Amber.

Through it all, Amber sat there, amazed and bewildered and overwhelmed. She'd gone to Turkey in search of finding some trace of her great-great-great-grandmother's trail, a taste of her adventure, and she'd found more than she'd ever imagined possible. She'd found a hint—the strongest possible hint—that her ancestor had been the Sultan's favourite.

And now she had the proof.

'Thank you,' she said, tears filming her eyes, 'for bringing these.'

'For God's sake, Amber, don't thank me. I was the one who took the bracelet from you in the first place. I called you a thief. I accused you of stealing it. I said horrible things to you that day.'

'Yes, you did,' she said, and he flinched, even though he knew it to be true. 'And I knew you'd find out the truth sooner or later. I just didn't know whether I'd be allowed to have it anyway, given its history and its age. I was beginning to think I'd never see it again.'

'I should never have taken it from you.'

'No.' She looked up at him, and raised herself to her feet. 'You shouldn't have. But I'm beyond happy to have it back. And now I have this too—' she held out the palm cradling the cameo '—and I feel like the mystery of where my great-great-great-grandmother disappeared to has finally been solved. Now I have more than an inkling of where she was and what she did. Now she is more real to me than ever. And yes, for that I thank you.'

He shook his head. 'Amber, I owe you an apology.'

She cut him off with a nod and a sweep of her hand. She'd been holding herself together, trying not to think about the way he'd treated her that last day. *Trying not to think about how he'd made love to her all the days and nights before that.* But she had her bracelet back and the bonus of the cameo besides. And now Kadar had done what he'd come here to do and the longer he stayed, the more painful it was, probably for them both. She didn't want to hear an explanation—she knew she'd given him cause to doubt her motives that very first day outside the Spice Market—and she suspected he really didn't want to have to give it. The best thing she could do was send him on his way. She gave a tight smile. 'Apology received and accepted. I'll show you to the door.'

She was already there and holding it open before he'd even moved a muscle.

'I'm not going anywhere,' he said.

And when she'd raised an eyebrow in question.

'Not before I tell you why I'm really here.'

CHAPTER FIFTEEN

Sensation sizzled through her.

'You've brought my bracelet back. I've accepted your apology. What else is there?'

'I have a confession. I was wrong about you.'

She shook her head and gestured towards the door. 'What part of "apology accepted" don't you understand? Please, Kadar, I don't want to listen to the whys and wherefores. I know why it happened and how. You had reason to doubt me from day one and you caught me what looked like red-handed. End of story.'

'No,' he said. 'It doesn't have to be.'

She swallowed and looked longingly towards his car. If he walked past her now Kadar would be gone in a few short seconds and she'd be free. Whatever it was he had to say, she didn't think she could bear it if it wasn't *that*.

She didn't know if she could bear it if it was. Her chest was tight and her palm slipped on the doorknob she still held in her hand.

'I don't know if I want to hear it.'

'Please. Hear me out,' he said, sounding like a man who'd reached the end of his tether and had nowhere else to go. 'And then I'll go if you want. But at least hear what I have to say.'

He was pleading with her, this man who had come

into her life ordering her around. And for the first time, Amber caught a glimpse of the child behind the man, a child who'd lost everything and suffered too much and had to grow up too fast. A child who had become a man who'd learned to shun people and relationships because he'd already lost more than one person could bear.

And he was here.

What did that mean? Her heart was tripping in her chest. She was almost afraid to breathe. 'Tell me,' she whispered.

He moved then. Finally. Moved towards her at the door until for a second she thought he'd changed his mind and decided to leave after all. But he stopped in front of her and took her hand, holding it almost reverently between his. 'You once said I had nothing to fear from you and I agreed,' he said. He looked into her eyes and she could see that he was as tightly wound as she felt. She could feel the tension in his long-fingered hands. 'I was wrong. I had everything to fear from you.

'Your smile, your eyes...' He lifted a hand to her face and ran his finger down the side of her cheek, a touch so featherlight—so missed—that she couldn't help but sigh as she leaned into it.

'From that first day in the Spice Market, I was doomed. And I tried to fight it—to fight you. I tried to keep you at a distance, to tell myself it was all duty. But I couldn't and it wasn't.

'And when you left—and when I found out what I'd done to you—it nearly broke me in two.'

She shook her head. 'And how do you think I felt? You called me a thief! You accused me of stealing my own bracelet!' Her voice was choking. She could not afford to forget about what he'd done to her, no matter how much her heart leaned towards his words as her face had leaned into his hand.

He dropped his head. 'I know.'

'So you don't have to say nice things now to try to make me feel better.'

He looked up. 'Is that what you think?'

'I don't know what to think, Kadar. You accuse me of being a thief and you take my bracelet and send me away like I'm a criminal, and then you turn up here and admit you were wrong and suddenly everything's supposed to be okay? No, everything's not okay.'

He swore under his breath. 'I am sorry, I am no good at this. What I am trying to say, Amber... What I came to tell you... I love you.'

She squeezed her eyes and her mind shut, refusing to give the tiny flutter in her heart oxygen. The words she'd most wanted to hear—once—before the door had been slammed shut in her face. 'You say that now.'

He dragged in a breath as he spun around and punched the air with his fist, before turning back to her. 'Do you have any idea what this was like for me? I wanted to say it before. The day you were leaving. I didn't want you to go. I wanted you to stay. I thought there might be a chance of us having a future together. I'd never done this before. I'd never thought it possible that I could love anyone. But you weren't like any other woman I'd ever met. You made me think the impossible was possible.'

She didn't move. She couldn't. It was all she could do to blink. And hope.

'Don't you understand? I had lost my family. I had defied my father and I had lived where they had died. I didn't deserve family. And then you came along, and made me wish for things that I had lost all hope of having.'

He sighed, and hung his head, shaking it slowly before he looked up, and the sorrow and regret in his eyes was almost too much for her to bear. 'I was about to tell you that. I was about to say the one thing I'd never been able to say to anyone in my life.

'And then I walked into that bedroom and saw you with the bracelet and that part of me that had fought getting close to you all along had found a reason why it could never work. I was furious with you, I know, but I was just even more furious with myself for falling for you.

'But when I discovered the truth and knew that I had lost you...' His voice trailed off, his dark, grief-filled eyes pleading with her as he took her hand, intertwining his fingers with hers. 'I know you have every right to tell me to get the hell out of that door and never come back. But I want to make it up to you. I want to make up for every wrong I committed against you, every day we're together, and every night.'

She blinked, her heart stalling for a long beat.

Follow your heart.

The words of Amber Braithwaite's faded inscription came back to her. And her mind might be telling her that she was crazy to consider ever forgiving this man for what he had done, but her heart was telling her that she would be a fool to let the man she loved walk away.

'What are you saying?' she whispered, keeping her voice even, afraid to show emotion in case she was wrong. 'Is the man who said he would never marry asking me to marry him?'

He slowly shook his head. 'I knew I had no right to

ask. I knew it would be impossible for you to love me after all that has happened.'

'Yes,' she said softly.

'I'm sorry,' he said on a sigh, sounding defeated. 'I have wasted your time, but I had to ask.'

'Kadar, I said yes.'

He frowned and it made her smile. 'I love you. I did my best to hate you, and I did, and more than a little. But it didn't stop me loving you. I don't know if it's possible to do that. I don't think it's something I can switch off like a tap. It's there and there's nothing, it seems, that I can do about it.'

'You love me, after everything that's happened?'

'I know,' she said, grinning now, because this supremely confident man had never looked more vulnerable or mortal. 'It's mad, but I do, and yes, I will marry you.'

And he growled like the Kadar of old as he swung the front door shut and collected her in his arms to kiss her.

His kiss was like coming home, his body hard and so familiar, warm and welcoming. With mouths and bodies meshed, she steered him to her room and her narrow single bed and as they peeled off their clothes they peeled away the layers of their past, all the wrongs and the misunderstandings and the pain, until there was nothing left but their love to bind them together.

EPILOGUE

THEY WERE MARRIED in Melbourne four months later, when the heat of the Australian summer had given way to the balmy days of autumn. Amber's father proudly waited to walk her down the aisle of the old Melbourne city church, Amber wearing a gown of lace that flared from the hips in a silk skirt that floated about her legs.

Kadar waited nervously, exchanging small talk with his best man, Rashid, and Amber's younger brother beside him. In the rows behind sat his friends, Zoltan and Bahir and their families. And finally, when he thought he could stand the waiting no longer, the music started, and he dragged in a deep breath. Rashid slapped him on the back. 'This is it,' he said, and Kadar turned.

One at a time Amber's two bridesmaids walked down the aisle, her two cousins, Tash's older sisters. He'd met them several times now, their names on the tip of his tongue, right until he saw the woman walking behind on her father's arm.

The woman he loved and there was only one name he could remember.

Amber.

She looked like a goddess in a gown that made her look as if she were floating down the aisle towards him, her blond hair coiled up high behind her head, her blue eyes sparkling and her smile wide as she nodded to the guests as she passed.

And on her wrist was the bracelet that had once graced a Sultan's favourite, the stones sparkling in their gold setting.

And then her eyes connected with his and it was as if she had flicked a switch as her face lit up, her smile electric, her eyes dazzling, and he knew he was the luckiest man alive.

'Beautiful,' he whispered to her as she joined him at the front. 'I love you.'

And she smiled and whispered back those words to him as the ceremony that would begin their lives together as man and wife got under way.

He was still holding hands with Amber while her mother and her friends hugged her, when Kadar's friends, Zoltan and Bahir, with their wives, Aisha and Marina, were the first to congratulate him after the ceremony. 'Another desert brother down,' said Zoltan. 'Bahir and I wondered how long it would take either of you two to come to your senses.'

'You sure made us wait long enough,' Bahir said.

Rashid joined his desert brothers and their wives. 'I guess this makes me the winner, huh?' and the three friends looked at each other and laughed.

'If you say so,' said Kadar.

His new wife joined the group. 'What's so funny?' she asked, and Kadar pulled her close and pressed his lips to her forehead. 'Rashid's funny.'

'Hey,' he said, 'just because you guys felt the need to get all domesticated and settle down, don't take it out on me.'

'You just wait,' said Zoltan.

'Yeah,' said Bahir, with a knowing smile. 'You won't know what's hit you.'

'I never saw it coming,' admitted Kadar as he pulled his new wife closer. 'So you better watch out.'

Rashid shook his head. 'I don't know, maybe I'm just wired differently from you guys.'

'Yeah,' said Kadar. 'Just keep telling yourself that.'

Around them children ducked and weaved through the crowd. Bahir and Marina's son and daughter, Chakir and Hana, now six and five, along with their two-year-old brother, Karim, trying to keep up, and behind him toddled Zoltan and Aisha's pigeon pair, only six months younger.

'This is the best day of my life,' Kadar told Amber later at the reception as he waltzed her around the dance floor.

'Mine too.' She smiled up at him. 'I'm only sorry Mehmet couldn't be here to witness it.'

'We'll see him next week,' he said. 'But he knows how happy we are. He knew you were right for me from the very beginning.'

'He was right. I love you, Kadar.'

His heart swelled so big, he wanted to howl at the moon. How could a man be so lucky?

'I love you, Amber.' And he kissed her sweetly on the lips and then he took her hand and pressed his lips to the bracelet that her great-great-great-grandmother had been given a century and a half before. The bracelet that had been given to the Sultan's favourite.

Because Amber was his favourite now, as she would be for ever.

* * * * *

*Look out for SHACKLED TO THE SHEIKH
the final instalment of
Trish Morey's DESERT BROTHERS series
Coming soon!*

MILLS & BOON®
Hardback – May 2015

ROMANCE

The Sheikh's Secret Babies	Lynne Graham
The Sins of Sebastian Rey-Defoe	Kim Lawrence
At Her Boss's Pleasure	Cathy Williams
Captive of Kadar	Trish Morey
The Marakaios Marriage	Kate Hewitt
Craving Her Enemy's Touch	Rachael Thomas
The Greek's Pregnant Bride	Michelle Smart
Greek's Last Redemption	Caitlin Crews
The Pregnancy Secret	Cara Colter
A Bride for the Runaway Groom	Scarlet Wilson
The Wedding Planner and the CEO	Alison Roberts
Bound by a Baby Bump	Ellie Darkins
Always the Midwife	Alison Roberts
Midwife's Baby Bump	Susanne Hampton
A Kiss to Melt Her Heart	Emily Forbes
Tempted by Her Italian Surgeon	Louisa George
Daring to Date Her Ex	Annie Claydon
The One Man to Heal Her	Meredith Webber
The Sheikh's Pregnancy Proposal	Fiona Brand
Minding Her Boss's Business	Janice Maynard

MILLS & BOON®
Large Print – May 2015

ROMANCE

The Secret His Mistress Carried	Lynne Graham
Nine Months to Redeem Him	Jennie Lucas
Fonseca's Fury	Abby Green
The Russian's Ultimatum	Michelle Smart
To Sin with the Tycoon	Cathy Williams
The Last Heir of Monterrato	Andie Brock
Inherited by Her Enemy	Sara Craven
Taming the French Tycoon	Rebecca Winters
His Very Convenient Bride	Sophie Pembroke
The Heir's Unexpected Return	Jackie Braun
The Prince She Never Forgot	Scarlet Wilson

HISTORICAL

Marriage Made in Money	Sophia James
Chosen by the Lieutenant	Anne Herries
Playing the Rake's Game	Bronwyn Scott
Caught in Scandal's Storm	Helen Dickson
Bride for a Knight	Margaret Moore

MEDICAL

Playing the Playboy's Sweetheart	Carol Marinelli
Unwrapping Her Italian Doc	Carol Marinelli
A Doctor by Day...	Emily Forbes
Tamed by the Renegade	Emily Forbes
A Little Christmas Magic	Alison Roberts
Christmas with the Maverick Millionaire	Scarlet Wilson

MILLS & BOON®
Hardback – June 2015

ROMANCE

The Bride Fonseca Needs	Abby Green
Sheikh's Forbidden Conquest	Chantelle Shaw
Protecting the Desert Heir	Caitlin Crews
Seduced into the Greek's World	Dani Collins
Tempted by Her Billionaire Boss	Jennifer Hayward
Married for the Prince's Convenience	Maya Blake
The Sicilian's Surprise Wife	Tara Pammi
Russian's Ruthless Demand	Michelle Conder
His Unexpected Baby Bombshell	Soraya Lane
Falling for the Bridesmaid	Sophie Pembroke
A Millionaire for Cinderella	Barbara Wallace
From Paradise...to Pregnant!	Kandy Shepherd
Midwife...to Mum!	Sue MacKay
His Best Friend's Baby	Susan Carlisle
Italian Surgeon to the Stars	Melanie Milburne
Her Greek Doctor's Proposal	Robin Gianna
New York Doc to Blushing Bride	Janice Lynn
Still Married to Her Ex!	Lucy Clark
The Sheikh's Secret Heir	Kristi Gold
Carrying A King's Child	Katherine Garbera

MILLS & BOON®
Large Print – June 2015

ROMANCE

The Redemption of Darius Sterne	Carole Mortimer
The Sultan's Harem Bride	Annie West
Playing by the Greek's Rules	Sarah Morgan
Innocent in His Diamonds	Maya Blake
To Wear His Ring Again	Chantelle Shaw
The Man to Be Reckoned With	Tara Pammi
Claimed by the Sheikh	Rachael Thomas
Her Brooding Italian Boss	Susan Meier
The Heiress's Secret Baby	Jessica Gilmore
A Pregnancy, a Party & a Proposal	Teresa Carpenter
Best Friend to Wife and Mother?	Caroline Anderson

HISTORICAL

The Lost Gentleman	Margaret McPhee
Breaking the Rake's Rules	Bronwyn Scott
Secrets Behind Locked Doors	Laura Martin
Taming His Viking Woman	Michelle Styles
The Knight's Broken Promise	Nicole Locke

MEDICAL

Midwife's Christmas Proposal	Fiona McArthur
Midwife's Mistletoe Baby	Fiona McArthur
A Baby on Her Christmas List	Louisa George
A Family This Christmas	Sue MacKay
Falling for Dr December	Susanne Hampton
Snowbound with the Surgeon	Annie Claydon

MILLS & BOON®

Why shop at millsandboon.co.uk?

Each year, thousands of romance readers find their perfect read at millsandboon.co.uk. That's because we're passionate about bringing you the very best romantic fiction. Here are some of the advantages of shopping at www.millsandboon.co.uk:

* **Get new books first**—you'll be able to buy your favourite books one month before they hit the shops

* **Get exclusive discounts**—you'll also be able to buy our specially created monthly collections, with up to 50% off the RRP

* **Find your favourite authors**—latest news, interviews and new releases for all your favourite authors and series on our website, plus ideas for what to try next

* **Join in**—once you've bought your favourite books, don't forget to register with us to rate, review and join in the discussions

Visit **www.millsandboon.co.uk**
for all this and more today!